Bright:
Being the Best You in a World of Less

{A Devotional Trio for Teens}

Sarah Humphrey

ISBN-13: 978-1724678379
ISBN-10: 172467837X

Table of Contents:

How to Take a Seflie:

A 30 Day Social Media #Detox to Regain Confidence and Connection

Butterflies & Blooms:

A Creative Devo for Tweens and Teens

Be YOU:

30 Practical Prayers for Living in your God-given Design

Dedicated to Ella and Lucy:
May You Always Shine Bright.
Love, Mama

How to Take a Selfie:

A **30 Day** Social Media #Detox to Regain
Confidence and Connection

Sarah Humphrey

To all the young girls in the world who deserve to know that they are *Beautiful.*

Hi. My name is Sarah, and I was a social media addict.

This is part of my teenage diary. Exaggerated? Maybe. Honest? Yes. Exposing what we've all thought from time to time but no one wants to say? Absolutely.

In these pages, I hope you find yourself. I have found me! It took a long time, a lot of thought, more tears than I would have liked, more honesty than I really would have liked, but more joy than I know what to do with!

We all want connection. We all want to be known. We all want to be loved. That is why He created us.

In a world whose hurts are highlighted by the electronic screens we peer into, where news stories often scare us, where at times our friends' Facebook feed scares us, and where true wholeness is needed, I hope exposing the irony of our situation will lead to fruitfulness.

I hope that in looking at ourselves, we can see what we emit, give away, and reflect. I desire that as we bring the phone up to our faces, we will be gracious and truthful about who we are and what we look like. I believe that we can accept the mercy to heal and the self-acceptance to rest. I write so that we can exude the pride that comes from knowing who we are and Whose we are. My goal is that we can look at ourselves through the lens of love.

In all things, I want us to care for ourselves. And, I do, hope we can take a picture of it.

#Sarah

How to Take a Selfie:
A **30 Day** #Detox to Regain Confidence and Connection

The Negative Side:
Wasting Time, Comparison, Addiction, Crippling Self-Esteem

Day 1: Waking Up
Day 2: Overwhelmed
Day 3: Expectations
Day 4: Emotional Overload
Day 5: Take a Selfie
Day 6: Confused
Day 7: Hopeless
Day 8: Angry
Day 9: Drama
Day 10: Wallowing

The Messy Middle:
Online Triggers, Recognizing Needs, Connecting with God, Receiving a New Story

Day 11: Detox
Day 12: Jealousy
Day 13: Comparison
Day 14: Bored
Day 15: Angry Again
Day 16: Performance-Acceptance
Day 17: Addiction
Day 18: Depression
Day 19: Social Anxiety
Day 20: Sober

The Positive Side:
Time Management, Getting Creative, Enjoying Relationship, Being a Light

Day 21: Clear
Day 22: Responses
Day 23: Create
Day 24: Decorate
Day 25: Excited
Day 26: Refreshed
Day 27: Grateful
Day 28: Choices
Day 29: Party Time
Day 30: Celebrate

The Breakdown: Practical Tools to Remember

Introduction

Selfies. You either love them or you hate them, there really hasn't been a great in-between space. In a world where our reflection matters, what young women (and women of all ages) want most is to feel comfortable in our own skin. We want self-acceptance, belonging, and the deep understanding that we are loved. We want to feel beautiful and to exude the courage to show up for our very own God-created destiny, and society gives us many ways to express that. We want to be recognized for who we are, what we love, and what we accomplish. We want our friends to see us, and we want to be celebrated. Yet peeling back the mask of shame, we often have a hard time fully connecting to our identity. There's a muddy space in the middle of where we want to be and where we are. We may get sidetracked by what we see of others, of what they are doing and experiencing and sharing with their world. We start to compare and contrast, get jealous or get even, we sometimes even forget what we really look like. Before we know it, an hour has passed.

And in the midst of this mind-game jungle, we hold a phone up to our face and we "click". Then we look deeper. Here is where we may start to sigh or invite self-hatred, ask for a do-over, or look away in disgust. Here we also might surprise ourselves and light up a bit, encouraged by what "faults" might not have been caught by the camera or what hue our eye color gleams that we never saw before.

It's the journey into the selfie. Who am I? What is my identity, where do I belong, and what do I do with my life? In a society where we are all trying so desperately to connect, we take a snapshot, share it, and wait for others to react. We also react to others, and take inventory of what we like and don't like.

Social media has quickly moved to the forefront of many of our daily interactions. It is used instead of coffee dates or real dates, always in the back of our mind for sharing our current experience with the world. As a culture, we want to feel known and loved. We want to share, be heard, and contribute, yet how we do that can either make us or break us.

What we send out into the world comes back to us; we desire to be salt and light. In this journey into ourselves, we must look at the bigger picture and journey into God. Jesus knew His identity, His purpose, and His mission. He didn't have Facebook but His face was never covered in shame. He could look right into the eyes of the Father with radiance.

God created women to exude beauty, to create, and to come together in community. His very desire for females was to express His nature by love, nurture, and communion. What we look for on the internet can be found in the quiet of stillness. What we may be missing in self-confidence is always waiting for us in the heart of God. What we lost to wounding can be cured by His presence. And when we take our face to God, He can make us shine.

As a return on our brilliance, we get to share, not out of lack but from overflow. In the connection of Presence, we fulfill our destiny. And in fullness, we take our story into the world. We share our authenticity, our heart, and our life. What we then find are those who needed a friend, those who can draw from our beauty, and those who can be encouraged by our triumph.

As we journey into identity, self-confidence, and belonging from the One who created us, we are freed to express ourselves to a world starving for the same. Social media becomes a conduit instead of a necessity; it becomes a bridge to bring hope instead of despair. It becomes a tool to share what we have learned with others who may need it.

So grab your Bible, a journal, and your iphone because what you hear from Him, you'll want to share. And post. And Tweet.

The Negative Side of Social Media:
Wasting Time, Comparison, Addiction, Crippling Self-Esteem

There is so much to be said about our current world of social media. Most of us have enjoyed the good and the bad, the connection and the disconnection, the joy and the absolute hatred of an online world. As screen time increases, our mental freedom often decreases. We find ourselves prone to an addiction to electronics, a life that is constantly available to interruption, emotions that can be difficult to navigate, and an array of opinions that might be better off unknown.

Social media is a force to be reckoned with now-a-days. It is a "Come to Jesus" meeting. What we see in ourselves because of how we are spending our time is plenty a topic to dialogue with God over. Electronic waves were never meant to replace light waves of sunshine and sound waves of nature; they were never meant to replace the touch of a human hand or the familiar scent of a friend's favorite perfume. We need connection, yes. But we probably need honesty first.

If we don't initiate the humble posture that is available to us in Christ, we may end up very sick before we actually change our lives. We are a culture that is sliding down the slippery slope of depression and anxiety, online addiction, and isolation. We have overstimulated introverts around every corner, friends who are taking their own lives because of online bullying, and children who are growing up on a screen.

Women, especially, are vulnerable to the woes of the internet as our beauty and worth is often threatened by the perceived beauty of another, the insta-success of the world around us, and the pressure to perform to an unattainable standard. It can often feel like we are not enough if we aren't performing in some way, if we feel less than in comparison to other friend's happenings, and if we can't take a professional selfie.

I think it's safe to assume we have all felt this way at one time or another. If life wasn't hard enough without online bullying or popularity contests, it is our reality now. All of those issues that matter without a screen only get amplified with a screen. We want to be connected, loved, and in community; this is why God designed us the way He did. And the first step toward revealing our humanity online, is to reveal our humanity in vulnerability. Let's take an honest look into our hearts. Let's allow ourselves the humility and the grace to be real. We all struggle; we all want to be known, and we all want to be nurtured. It is the way of redemption.

As we journey into the life of a modern day teenager and her relationship with social media—in the midst of throwing her own birthday party, let's also look into ourselves and how we might ask God to heal our hearts of a system that has, at times, led us astray. Let's ask Him to give us grace and mercy for the wholeness and community we naturally need.

17

Day 1: Waking Up

I wake up with an ache in my back after a rough night's sleep. Trying to get myself out of bed, I look at my nightstand. And there's my relief, the smartphone, just lingering and looking at me. Waiting for me. Instead of rolling over or just waking up, I unplug it from the charger and snuggle back into bed. The bright light from the screen makes my just-opened eyes squint, but it takes away the ache from early morning. Instagram, email, Facebook, Twitter. Who has liked my posts? Who said this or that? Who saw me? What can I see?

This is how I start my day. Connected to a screen, connected to a dream—of being known. Belonging. Contributing to a conversation or just watching one form while taking a backseat. Categorizing these relationships with likes and agrees—or building walls in my heart when others express themselves differently than me. I can take the microphone and shout, be a peacemaker and gently try to persuade, or sit quietly in the background risking nothing but judging everything.

It's how life works these days. And if you aren't on the grid, you're one of the few. Society is on their phones—connecting and disconnecting at the same time. So I'm taking an inventory of myself, of who I am, what I believe, and what I do. How am I recognized, and what is my value doing for my online community? What is it doing for myself? And my family and friends? Is it contributing to or taking away from my time? Do I like my selfie, or do I cringe in despair?

Examine me, God! Look at my heart!
Put me to the test! Know my anxious thoughts!
Look to see if there is any idolatrous way in me,
Then lead me on the eternal path.
Psalm 139: 23-24

Connecting Questions: How do I start my day? How much time do I spend on social media daily? Is screen time a potential issue for me?

Day 2: Overwhelmed

Today is one of those days without wind in my sails. Feeling a bit overwhelmed and under-started in life. There always seems like there is more to do than time to do it. I have my own birthday party to plan and no mojo to get going. Too many ideas popping into my head, so much to manage, so much I don't really want to look at. It sounds like the perfect time to procrastinate. I wonder what's happening on Facebook? I'll just go on for a few minutes to clear my mind before I get started on my party planning.

Click, and scroll...
OH MY GOSH! That is hilarious! I'm going to have to share that. I bet my friends will get a kick out of that. What can I say that's witty to add to it? And....post.

Scroll...
Ewwww. I can't believe she posted that. I wouldn't say something like that in public. How embarrassing. Keep moving.

Scroll...
Awe! That's so cute. I wish I had something like that. "Like."

Scroll...
Why doesn't my hair look that good? Where did she get her lipstick?

Scroll...
BLEEP. BLEEP. BLEEP. Geez, please watch your mouth. Everything you post has a bad word in it.

Scroll...
And a half hour has passed. I better get to work.

But, seriously, I'm so overwhelmed and under-started. How do I get going now? I have too many ideas, too many thoughts running through my head. I've seen too much. I wish I could un-see that. I think I might need to get something for my anxiety. Something's not right with me. Maybe I just need some medication. Or maybe I just need a friend, someone to connect with. I really could use some advice on how to get started. Maybe I'll just go on Instagram and see what so and so is doing. She always seems to have some good ideas...

God didn't give us a spirit that is timid but one that is powerful, loving, and self-controlled.
2 Timothy 1:7

Connecting Questions: Do you use social media to procrastinate? Is there anything specific you're procrastinating on? What is it? Why are you waiting?

Day 3: Expectations

Ok! Today's plan is to focus. I was not focused yesterday; today I'm centered. I'm going to get stuff done. First things first, I need to get my birthday party planned and then get off the internet. Pinterest, I'll start with you! Somebody post a good theme and some recipes, and I'll be good to go. Mexican theme, sombreros, tacos, piñata....perfect!

Scrolling...

Oh my gosh. That's a really intense party. I wonder if I have to make all that? You think people will expect that? Are they really IN Mexico? Maybe there is something similar with not quite so much pizazz. But are people expecting that pizazz? What if I can't do that much? Will people be disappointed? How much is this going to cost? Should I ask my mom to hire a person to do the hosting for me?

Ok, I'm totally overwhelmed. I don't know if I can compare to what is posted here. I really need to know what other people's expectations are going to be. What are my expectations? I don't know if I can compare to this internet world. I don't know if I have the help to do this. Should I just charge it on my mom's credit card? Maybe I should just cancel the party; no one will know the difference and then I can just hide. Did I just say that out loud?

I think I have social anxiety. Maybe I should just stick to the internet world. Less face time and less to stress about. My expectations stay low, I don't have to spend the time or energy, and I don't have to compare myself. But if I don't throw the party, what will I have to post? There will be no pictures of happiness or awesomeness!! What will people think of me then?

I just don't know if I'm doing enough. I just don't know if I can handle the stress of doing enough. I think I have a comparison issue. I don't even know how to throw a party. I don't even know WHO I AM!

I know the plans I have in mind for you, declares the LORD; they are plans for peace, not disaster, to give you a future filled with hope.
Jeremiah 29:11

Connecting Questions: Do you have unfair expectations of yourself? Do you compare yourself to others often? How? What, if anything, makes you consider yourself not enough?

Day 4: Emotional Overload

The party is on its way! Slowly but surely, I'm moving. Now, who to invite? I can just text or do a Facebook invitation. How big do I want this party to be? Because if this friend sees that I invited that friend and not her, then feelings are going to get hurt. People will post pictures, so she's going to find out. But if the party is too big, my parents won't pay for it. Can I tell people at the party not to post any pictures on Facebook? But that's no fun! No one will see what a great party I'm having and all the fun people that came. If I invite everyone I want to, then I will have to make less snacks per person and focus more on music and activities.

I don't even know if I'm doing this right. I don't even know which friends I want to include. Is anyone else feeling overwhelmed or just me? I'm sweating. Jesus, help me, I'm sweating. My heart is beating so fast; I don't want to offend anyone. I want to make sure I have enough for my friends to do at my party. I want people to take pictures of my party and share it because I AM FUN, darnnit! And it's my BIRTHDAY! I am POPULAR, ok?!?!

I need to calm down. I'm gonna go scroll.

"Crazy lady in grocery store knocks over 30 bottles of mouthwash in Walmart". Click.

"Homeless man arrested for sleeping outside a local coffee shop." Click.

"Riots in the street. Shootings continue." Click.

"Online addiction-a generation with depression and anxiety." Click.

That's it.

Status Update: *How do you feel?:*

"You want to know how I FEEL? I'm sick of this! Our world is crazy! People are crazy! I'm over here about to have a panic attack over a party. First world problems. Somebody like this before I hyperventilate!"

(30 LIKES)
Comments:

You really should calm down. It's not a good idea to be so angry on social media.

Are you ok? Do you want me to bring you something?

Praise Jesus from whom all blessings flow. Focus on God, dear child.

That's right! THIS WORLD STINKS!!!!!!!!!!!!!

And.......sign off for now. Go breathe.

The peace of Christ must control your hearts—a peace into which you were called in one body.
Colossians 3:15

Connecting Questions: Does social media take away or contribute to your confidence? What is the most common trigger on social media that steals your peace?

Day 5: Take a Selfie

Ok, let's cross a few things off my "To Do" list. Send out the invitation to friends. Check. Fill yourself with good thoughts, girl. You've got this. You can delete that other crazy status update. It's happened to all of us at one time or another. No one will judge. Who I am I kidding? Most people will judge. But it's OK. Everyone makes mistakes. We all just need to let it go every once and awhile. It's going to be ok. Put on a new shade of lipstick, send out those e-invitations, and you've got this.

And done. I did it! The party is on its way! Now, get on with living. Take a picture of this! You did it. Look at you!

(Fix hair a bit, and add a little bit of lip gloss. Turn phone around. Smile, and click. Take another. One more....and back to the Original. Edit. Find a filter. Adjust the light.....that's about right. Write something witty. Erase. Write something else. Add an emoticon. Ask a friend if it sounds ok. Does it look ok? Do I look like I'm trying too hard? Breathe. And post.)

Hold my breath, wait....wait....wait. Somebody please like it before I delete it....wait....wait....and THANK YOU! THANK YOU! THANK YOU! You saved my life! And b-r-e-a-t-h-e.....maybe even laugh a little. And maybe even cry.

And there it is, a tear.

I've had so much pent up emotion. There's so much I want to express and so many ways to do it. I just want to feel connected to myself. I'm trying to funnel all of this passion inside me. I just want to be who I was created to be and help other people have some fun.

But you are a chosen race, a royal priesthood, a holy nation, a people who are God's own possession. You have become this people so that you may speak of the wonderful acts of the one who called you out of darkness into his amazing light.
1 Peter 2:9

Connecting Questions: Have you ever taken a selfie? How did it make you feel? Do you find yourself better or worse when looking at your picture?

Day 6: Confused

I should feel on top of the world. Did you see all the likes? So many people celebrated my selfie, told me how good I looked, and yet....I wrestle. I don't know if I feel better or if in some weird way, I feel worse. I'm not sure if what people celebrate about me is what I really see in myself or if that is really who I am. I wanted the likes, and I wanted the affirmation, but what am I affirming exactly? My hair? My looks? My confidence? My style? Somewhere in the mix of the anxiety to fit in, I almost feel like an outsider. I'm trying to plan a party, I'm trying to include, I'm trying to have fun and feel connected and celebratory and alive. But somewhere I've taken a detour. I'm no longer feeling anxious but slowly feeling depressed. What does this mean? What does it matter? Does any of this matter? Who cares about throwing parties? Who cares about being seen? I-hate-it-all. Maybe I should just give up on trying to fit in. Maybe I need quiet. Maybe my needs aren't so much about being seen but ultimately being known. I get so overwhelmed by trying to fit all of my expressions into one box—the internet. I'm trying to prove myself on a profile, but I haven't seen myself in real life. Have you ever noticed that selfies look nothing like what you look like in the mirror?

I don't even want to go near my phone.

I don't even want to think about what other people are doing.

I don't even care. I'm angry at a selfie that I took myself and people said they liked.

What is wrong with this picture? Literally.

> *Why, I ask myself, are you so depressed?*
> *Why are you so upset inside?*
> *Hope in God!*
> *Because I will again give him thanks,*
> *My saving presence and my God.*
> *Psalm 43:5*

Connecting Questions: Have you ever felt badly after posting a picture or thought on the internet? Where do you go when your hope for connection fails?

Day 7: Hopeless

Everything feels a bit hopeless today. A few people have responded to the party invitation, so I guess that's good. I could start gathering my supplies, but I just don't know that I feel like it right now. Two of my guests aren't really getting along right now, so I'm not sure exactly what I'm going to do. One of them made the other mad, and now my Facebook feed is filled with passive aggressive memes about each of their processes. Then, of course, people start taking sides. It's kind of like mind games. There's so much friction between them, so much being thrown into the atmosphere, but there really isn't any understanding. I wonder if it's really the best way for them to communicate, or if they should both be alone for awhile. If this keeps up, people are going to start talking. "Did you see what so and so posted? She is mad." But did you see what her friend wrote in response? She's not having any of it!" Ugh. I'm kind of dreading having to face these two in real life. I don't know if it's just going to be awkward conversation or if they'll pretend like nothing is wrong and just keep it under wraps while hating each other from a distance. I mean, I've done it before. I've gotten mad at people's posts, only to breathe fire at my phone screen and then smile the next time I see them.

Sometimes I wonder if we all just need a little quiet time, a break from one another? But we're all so desperate to be friends. How does that work? We are attracted to the very thing that makes us anxious, angry, and upset. We hate what we see, and in turn, start hating each other. But when we're face-to-face, we really don't know how to talk. We still just look at our screens.

I hope my party isn't a whole night of people looking at their phones.

There are persons for companionship,
But then there are friends who are more loyal than family.
Proverbs 18:24

Connecting Questions: Have you ever fought with a friend over social media? What are some productive ways to filter communication in disagreements?

Day 8: Angry

I'm SO MAD right now! I just found out that my so called friend is hosting a party the same night I am! She invited almost all of the same people, and I know that they are going to end up at her party instead of mine (#selfpity). I wonder if she did this to try to hurt my feelings? Or did she not even see my post? She had to have seen my post; I sent her an invite, and she knows it's my birthday! I don't know if she answered the notification though. Maybe she didn't see it, BUT MAYBE SHE DID, and she copied me. Should I call her and say something? Should I send her a nasty text and stand my ground? Or should I just delete my party and pretend like it never happened? I'm going to her Facebook page to see what she's been saying.

Scrolling…

It looks like other people have been commenting on all her stuff. I wonder if they are talking behind my back. I only have a few people who have confirmed coming to my party. Wait, someone just changed from a "Yes" to a "Maybe"! I bet they were invited to hers and are going! I'm going to go look at her invitation if I can. Why wouldn't she invite me? Maybe it was just a mistake, and she's still inviting people. Maybe I'll get a notification later today. I'll just keep checking back before I say anything. I don't want to get too worked up, but I am already worked up! What if people like me online but don't really care about me in person? Does that mean we are even really friends?

What is a friend anymore? I hate high school.

> **As iron sharpens iron,**
> **So friends sharpen each other's faces.**
> **Proverbs 27:17**

Connecting Questions: Have you ever seen a friend interaction online that made you feel less than? How did you handle it?

Day 9: Drama

Gossip, jealousy, and eavesdropping. That is my what online life has become. I'm feeding my own drama. I'm looking for something to look at, something to make me feel better about myself, something to serve me. Who knew that all of this would come up simply trying to make something good happen? All I've wanted is connection. I've just been hoping to create a place where I can belong, where I can feel good about myself, where I can be with others, and where I can contribute to a convo in a fun way. I've just wanted to bring people into my personality, open myself up to being a little bit brave but also be able to shut the door when I want to. I guess that's the internet. I didn't expect planning a party in real life would bring up so much in myself that I wasn't prepared to deal with. I didn't realize I had all of these self-confidence and comparison issues, that inviting people to show up in real life was so much different than having them "like" my post.

I didn't know that I would feel so left out when someone didn't answer a friend request or never liked one of my photos. I didn't know how badly it felt to be left out until I constantly see other people together with pictures of how they are "in". I think I need a social media detox. If I feel this way, I need to figure out what is going on. From anxiety to the blues to plain old being ignored (or maybe I'm overreacting), I'm just over it. I'm going to start a social media detox tomorrow. I can't do it today; I'm not prepared for that. Let me just wallow and see if an invite shows up; if it does, maybe I won't need to unplug.

Therefore, as God's choice, holy and loved, put on compassion, kindness, humility, gentleness, and patience. Be tolerant with each other and, if someone has a complaint against anyone, forgive each other. As the Lord forgave you, so also forgive each other. And over all these things put on love, which is the perfect bond of unity.
Colossians 3:12-14

Connecting Questions: Have you ever done a social media detox? What triggered you into realizing it was necessary?

Day 10: Wallowing

Waiting, waiting, waiting...

Waiting, waiting, waiting...

Wallowing, wallowing......wal-low-ing...

I don't think anyone is coming for me. I think I need to help myself. Maybe they forgot about me? Maybe it was an accident? Maybe they can't read my mind? Maybe I just don't fit in. So, I guess it's time to find out who I am. How can I connect with myself? How can I move through all of these feelings and hurts and thoughts that keep bringing me up one day and down the next day?

Being connected to a screen for relationship is turning me into a crazy person. Without having a real conversation, I don't see a person's facial expressions or body language or heart. Virtual hugs are fine, but what I really want is a friend. I want a human being to look at and touch, someone to listen and someone to respond, not by way of typing but by actually seeing my heart.

So, here goes nothing.

Status Update: How do you feel?

"Hey guys! I'm taking a week or so off social media to refresh my brain! If you try to message me here, I won't get it until next week. Call or text me if you need to get ahold of me! Xoxo"

One like, two likes, three likes, four likes........and counting.

I guess I'm not the only one.

Time for a good cry in the girls' room. Good night, internet.

So you see that a Sabbath rest is left open for God's people. The one who entered God's rest also rested from his works, just as God rested from his own.
Hebrews 4:9-11

Connecting Questions: What is your favorite way to get quiet from the internet? What builds your inner strength?

The Messy Middle:
Online Triggers, Recognizing Needs, Connecting with God, Receiving a New Story

It's true that social media has its place in society; in fact, we can't ignore it. The internet is here, and it doesn't look like it is going anywhere any time soon. What do we do with our online triggers? What do we do when we spend our days communicating with a screen but without real connection and community with real people? How do we live in a natural life and filter what goes into an online profile? How do we connect and find our identity in a world that is constantly giving us outlets to perform and project but less and less opportunity to be authentic and real face-to-face?

We don't want to alienate ourselves from culture; we can live in this world but not be of the world. Jesus only resorted to isolation when it was time to pray. And pray, we must. We also don't want to resort to bitterness, jealousy, gossip, and anger when we see or hear something that may have been better left unsaid. And even if that something needed to be said, we also need to learn proper boundaries and how to turn our own triggered hurts and wounds into wholeness. If we want to stay in sync with a modern world, we have to learn how to juggle the online world. We need to learn connection and wholeness from a place of prayer and oneness with God.

When these areas creep up in our lives because of what we see others doing, it is the perfect time to slow down. Emotions are a compass that leads us to God. How did that make me feel? Angry? Less than? Stupid? Unheard? Ugly? Flattered? Defiled? It's true that social media has just as many positives as negatives. It can also make us feel loved, known, cherished, appreciated, seen, and validated. The key that lies before us is trading in the broken for the beautiful. We want to give our hurts a voice, but in a proper platform, so that our words can bring unity instead of division. We want to use what we've learned to be a light to others. We want to connect. Sometimes a short detox is needed to regroup, reclaim, and reinvent ourselves. It's good to feel; it's also good to exercise self-control. It's good to see; it's also good to rest. It's good to be in online community; it's also good to be present with others without an electronic device. Sometimes what we need is just a good cry; that's one of the best reasons for a girls' bathroom. Let it out, re-group, powder that cute face, and be on our way out the door.

It's in the messy middle that we find ourselves. Our triggers are evident and can be well-documented in the chaos. What we do with those triggers determines our health and our future. Let's have that good cry. It's worth it.

Day 11: Detox

When I sit down with myself, and I have to wonder, "What is happening to me?", I know that I need a detox. I'm so looking forward to the quiet, hearing myself speak, and writing out the feelings of my heart. How often is it that I acknowledge myself? Not in a status update but truly and deeply acknowledge myself? In times of overwhelm, where emotions run high and my body gets weak, there is only one thing that will heal: absolute presence in God. God has never left, ever. But I leave him. Every time I agree with an untrue thought, any time I dishonor myself, and every time I believe a lie. It not only hurts me, it hurts Him. It hurts Him not because He is angry at me or because He wishes I wouldn't mess up so badly or because I've disappointed Him. Absolutely not. It hurts Him because He misses my presence, my quiet and my acceptance before Him. It grieves Him because He loves me, has already made a way for my passion and my heart and my destiny, and He loves to provide the tools to see me succeed. He is for me. He created the selfie. Light and joy on my face are reflections of His. And so I have needed this time to reconnect with "us". It's refreshing to know that a God so good can allow me the freedom to choose. He gives me creativity and gives me passion, He wants me to have friends, and He wants me to influence others. He also wants me to believe in my beauty, not because I need to saturate a world with a selfie but because He and I together can load up the clutter left behind, and we can glue, and paint, and restore it to it's very original existence. It's part of the privilege we have, of being together. When I get too caught up in my insecurity, trusting too much in my time away from Him or trying to get to Him, I lose sight of Him. And, so, social media, I thank you for the wake-up call. I won't blame you or berate you for what I can own myself. I'm free to repent of where I've gone wrong, of where I've used you for comfort, and where I've lost myself in the way of EMF waves. Here's to silence, and cheers to a few days unplugged. May I be saturated in truth and grace, not only for myself, but also to share.

My body and my heart fail,
But God is my heart's rock and my share forever.
Psalm 73:26

Connecting Questions: Where have I left God's presence? Where do I need to repent, start over, or rest?

30

Day 12: Jealousy

I've been thinking through the components that make me scrunch my nose and burn in my belly. What is with those pictures of others' celebrations that can make me feel a little sick in my stomach and unable to extend a "Like"? Where is it that my heart gets hardened and my back wants to turn away?

Jealousy; you play tricks on me.

As if celebrating someone else will make my life worse somehow, I think I've seen way too many other people having parties while I have pitied myself. It's true, suffering has come to me. And in suffering, there is room for solace. But there is always room for joy. What is it about watching someone else succeed in her world that can turn a friend into an enemy? When someone gets what I want? Is what I want all used up now? Or is it just burning in my belly because I wasn't first? Is winning what I want? What is it that I am truly after? Honor? Being adored? Praise from others? Or do I really want connection with myself? Do I really want self-acceptance and peace? Praise from the lips of a crowd may feel good in a moment, but true agreement with my identity in faith and in works is where I really long to be. Those missing parts of me that are crying to be matched up, healed, and put beautifully put back together, that is what I'm after. I should never be distracted by just that, the distraction. My goal is to find the root. Who is the root? He is.

So today I offer up my jealousy. May the gifts, talents, and celebrations of others be blessed. And let that start with my agreement and with my "like".

Wherever there is jealousy and selfish ambition, there is disorder and everything that is evil.
James 3:16

Connecting Questions: Are there specific areas in your life that are triggered by social media jealousy? Who might you be jealous of? Why? What is it that you would like to connect with inside yourself?

31

Day 13: Comparison

Comparison, you silly little lie. You make me think I'm less than, you size me up to others, you always leave me feeling inadequate. Even if I think of myself as better, you really just try to prove that I am less. And as you dribble your lies through my self-worth, I start to believe that the appearance of things can heal the gaps of my soul, but I always come back to the same feeling: emptiness. What is it about looking at someone and then looking at myself that can make me cower my head in shame or puff my chest up in pride? How do you compare two immaculate beings? How do you dare try to choose one of God's creations as better or worse? Where has my heart gone that I would look at myself and think less than or look at a friend and portray less than over her?

You are thief.

And a bully.

You hide in my insecurity, in the gaps that Jesus loves to love. I'm no longer giving you a place. I will not look at myself and compare me to someone else. I will not compare my face or my life; I will not compare my schoolwork or my looks. I will not compare my gifts or my talents. No more stealing. No more less than. No more more than.

Today I'm giving up comparison. I give my self-esteem to Jesus. I give my worth and my convictions, my story and my life into the hands that have given everyone the same value. No longer will I succumb to you; and if I forget, may God give me the grace to turn-around quickly.

Each person should test their own work and be happy with doing a good job and not compare themselves with others. Each person will have to carry their own load.
Galatians 6:4-5

Connecting Questions: What are your most common causes for comparison? How can you give yourself care in an area where you'd like to grow personally?

Day 14: Bored

It's been three days so far. I wonder what everyone is doing…..

I guess I need to know what everyone else is up to because I get bored in life. Every inkling of dissatisfaction is quickly pushed aside into the internet world. Bored? Check Facebook. Go see what everyone else is doing to keep busy. Why is it always easier to watch than it is to put in the effort of creating?

I choose to be bored. I choose to watch instead of do.

How many minutes a day could I spend producing joy instead of watching others "experience" it? Or watching others completely disregard it?

If we get to live just one life, how do I want to spend my time? It seems that staring at a screen and vicariously relaxing through the stories of others wouldn't be the best way to live a life. Doesn't that seem silly? Out of all that time, I could be creating, moving, cooking, drawing, building, or even cleaning my room for goodness sake! Wouldn't I rather have clean and creative space for myself instead of a body that has absorbed too much electricity?

This is profound to me.

Why did I never understand this about myself? I am bored, but I am not needy. I can create. I can do. I can choose better than saturating myself in the audience. This is my life to live; I want to choose to experience people and places and culture in real time, not on a screen.

Today I'm giving up "people watching" over the internet. There is a difference between connection and procrastination. I want to live with passion not with lack of desire.

> *The lazy have strong desires but receive nothing;*
> *The appetite of the diligent is satisfied.*
> *Proverbs 13:4*

Connecting Questions: What is your most common excuse for procrastination? List three things you can do in the time you use checking your phone.

Day 15: Angry Again

You know what makes me angry? People who have different opinions than me who plaster them all over my social media feeds. Over and over again. This-makes-me-angry. You know what else makes me angry? People who are mean in every meme. You know what else makes me angry? Half-naked pictures of girls for sale; why do people do that to girls? You know what else makes me angry? My friends being hurt by online bullying.

I don't even know if I should get started! Because if I get started, I might not know how to slow down and control myself. If someone takes me over the edge, I may forget that I am a Christian at all. I may just get my fingers tapping really loudly and then erasing and then tapping again, my lips tight and my chest burning like a flame of fire. If I'm lucky, I'll get interrupted. If I'm lucky, I'll remember who God is. If I'm lucky, I will STOP MYSELF before those words get etched onto an electronic platform that can be deleted but rarely erased from my mind—or someone else's.

Where can I get out my anger? How do I deal with my hurt feelings? How do I fix things that are wrong? What do I do when my heart wants to scream but my mind says: "Don't say that." What do I do when a cause needs shared but I don't want to be like a lot of other screaming people on the interwebs? I'm still figuring this out—how to understand myself.

No body has really been able to tell me how to be angry and how to deal with feeling alone. What I do know is that when I'm angry that means my boundaries have been crossed. And if I feel betrayed, then it very well might be time for me to make some new boundaries.

This is where I learn to control my myself and walk away. There are few arguments on the internet that help; why do I see so many adults fighting on the internet? I want to find the people in life who want to make the world better. The art of expressing disgust without a need to repent later is still escaping me, so for now I'll just ask God to bring me to my knees. I am in need of help. I need your Holy Spirit, and I need your fruit of self-control. Be with me, God, as I navigate the emotion that often leads me to regret.

Know this, my dear brothers and sisters: everyone should be quick to listen, slow to speak, and slow to grow angry. This is because an angry person doesn't produce God's righteousness.
James 1:19-20

Connecting Questions: What are your most common triggers for anger? What can you choose as a healthy management outlet? Are there people in your friends' list you may need to block or take a break from?

Day 16: Performance-Acceptance

You know what really gets me feeling down? Thinking that I have nothing going on in my life if I have nothing to post online. There's a path to greatness, to sharing what is inside you, to giving the world your best, but it seems like everyone is performing all the time. Why is it that everyone wants to be seen but not many people want to have depth? There always seems to be mixture everywhere; and I'm still learning how to be myself without performing as "someone". There is a difference between being and acting, between expressing and asking for attention, and between sharing and luring. Social media has only increased our attraction to perform. Anyone can now have a reality show or a platform or a place to say something, but doesn't leadership mean being responsible? Anything that comes out on the computer can be criticized, and if it isn't coming from my heart but from my shadow, will it really work?

I want depth. I want to give from my heart and not from a place of need. I want to be my true self not try to act like my true self. I can't fake it until I make it. I want to be made. I want to be re-created in my own skin, I want to be born again. If it is Jesus within me that creates, I want to understand this. Who am I in light of Him? Who has He made me to BE? How do I shine from the inside out instead of attracting worth from the outside in? Who am I when no one is watching? Integrity is more valuable than success. Wholeness is always more effective than shortchanging myself. I want to be full. I want to overflow and not pretend.

Integrity guides the virtuous,
But dishonesty ruins the treacherous.
Proverbs 11:3

Connecting Questions: What hinders your depth? Who are you when no one is watching? Do you like what you see? What do you want to change?

Day 17: Addiction

A generation of addicts can only be healed by the stillness and presence of God. What propels us to instant gratification steals the peace we actually long for. It's been quiet, and I have actually heard myself ask for noise. It's almost as if we have become addicted to chaos. The sounds of the world have muffled their way into every inch of our lives. We need to know what is going on at all times. We need to be available at all times. We need the high of a notification or a text message to feel connected in a world that has continually left us broken. If it isn't drugs or alcohol, it is easily the internet and what it offers. It is connection and the need to be needed. It is wanting to be known, wanting to fulfill the purpose for which we were born, and it is wanting to know who we are in this big, messy world. In one way, I see friends perform. If we do well, we are seen and appreciated. In another way, I see friends rebel. We will not be talked down to or controlled, and we do not want to be forced out of our own will. What we don't seem to have in family or other friendships, we just make up online. I need my family and friends; I was made for community and sharing and being with others. And what does this look like when the computer can replace being real? How do I move back into silence and be real again in community? How can I say "I need you" to the people I love the most?

We need the connection, yes. We need to know that we are deserving of love and attention and care. We need to set boundaries and move toward natural life, where we can look into each other's eyes and share real time. We need to know the comfort of human touch again, not just the tapping of a screen or having our faces hidden under a profile.

> *The Lord replied, "I'll go myself, and I'll help you."*
> *Exodus 33:14*

Connecting Questions: How can you incorporate 20 minutes of silence and prayer into your daily life? Who can you invite out for a coffee date? Where do you need to set a boundary with the "noise" of your life?

Day 18: Depression

What is the major source of sadness in my life? This is really important to look into. If what I want to portray on the screen or at my party is real joy, what is the root of all that keeps me down? What keeps me inflamed and slow and stuck-in-the-sludge? Is it a lack of creativity? Or a lack of friends? Or the lack of a real life?

What do I do in my free time? Does screen time take over exercise time? If I'm sedentary, will I ever get moving? If all I do is watch others, I only seem to pick up what they are doing but don't seem to release anything inside of me. It's easy to become depressed when jealousy, judgement, and eavesdropping control me. It's easy to feel down when the whole world seems to be moving, but I seem to just sit in the stands like an outsider.

Get moving. Get going. A life waits outside the computer screen! Take all the stress and the un-comfort and be on the way to doing something great. Everything needed for a good and fun life is already inside my heart; He has kept it there from the very beginning. If I don't unpack it, I will always be grieved. If I don't have a life, I will always be sad. I will always be "behind". I will always fall short. Real love is expressed best in motion. When we are free to just be with God, then we are free to truly do. Don't stay in a cage. A canvas of life awaits full of hope and creativity and motion. Hop away from the screen, and go create your dream!

> *Don't fear, because I am with you;*
> *Don't be afraid, for I am your God.*
> *I will strengthen you,*
> *I will hold you*
> *With my righteous strong hand.*
> *Isaiah 41:10*

Connecting Questions: What are two hobbies you have wanted to try but haven't? How can you get 10 minutes of exercise today?

Day 19: Social Anxiety

It's interesting to connect with people again. I've been watching my body language and my interactions. I am nervous to be with people. I'm so used to writing a text or being in a posted picture. My introvert nature has ruled my social life. The computer screen has been my access to friendship. And now when I connect with others, I can truly start to feel myself. I feel nervous. Do I make eye contact? My heart is beating fast. I keep apologizing. I feel spacy. It's whirlwind living. Awkward conversation awaits.

But I am learning to push through. Does she feel weird like me? I keep shifting in my seat. I'm trying to get comfortable, trying to feel secure. Having a friendship in the outside world requires some faith. I realize I'm more anxious than I know, perhaps too self-aware and very sensitive to my surroundings. My nerves are tingly, and my blood moves quickly.

I don't know if I've ever not had social anxiety; the internet has always been around. That seems to be how we are gain social skills. Sometimes I feel like I almost know too much about people and then wonder if they know too much about me, but it feels weird to talk about it in person. Knowing so much on a screen but lacking so much confidence in real life. I'm wondering if anyone else feels this way? Like bravery is for hiding behind a typed word, and what we would never say or do in person is what we almost always do on the internet?

This is socially weird. This makes me not trust people. This makes me not trust myself.

Throw all your anxiety onto him, because he cares about you.
1 Peter 5:7

Connecting Questions: What is my most honest fear when connecting face to face instead of online? What people skills did you once have that might be lacking because of too much technology? What do you need to implement in your face to face interactions that you're not afraid to say or do online?

Day 20: Sober

It's been 10 days now without social media. I feel good, like I've gone deep in my own mind. I feel like I've asked myself a lot of questions that were needed. The lack of apps on my phone has given me more freedom to make a mental note of when I reach for it. The first few days of detox, I reached all the time. When I picked it up, I remembered it didn't exist. And then I had to sit down with myself and think:

Why am I going to my phone right now?

What emotion is the most present?

What am I going to the internet for that I could find more of in Jesus?

Who does God want to be for me right now?

How do I allow Him the space in my life to be that?

This is good. I feel good. I feel honest and connected in my heart. Even though I feel a little nervous going back to cyber world, I feel ahead of my own game. I am aware and awake, and I won't go backwards. My places of insecurity are slowly being melted away by the power of true connection. My identity is being shaped by my story of intimacy with God. My life online can now be a representation of what I've received instead of what I need.

I'm looking forward to going back to my friendships online tomorrow. There have been people I've missed. I'm curious about what's going on in their lives because I really do love them. I want to know because I care, but I'll no longer let a text or FB comment replace a real conversation. I'm going to start talking more at school and meeting people more to hang out. I'm going to start creating more. I'm looking forward to sharing that with the world.

But for one more day, I'll enjoy this life unplugged.

Yes, you will go out with celebration,
And you will be brought back in peace.
Even the mountains and the hills will burst into song before you;
The trees of the field will clap their hands.
Isaiah 55:12

Connecting Questions: What are the benefits you've gained from quiet? What can you look forward to sharing on social media?

The Positive Side of Social Media:
Time Management, Getting Creative, Enjoying Relationship, Being a Light

After spending just ten days unplugged, it's amazing what silence can do for a chaotic mind. It's in these moments of solitude and communion with God that we actually get to hear who we are. While on the internet, we may see a glimpse of who we would like to be or what we would like to do, and that is not always a bad thing. In God's presence we can develop our idea into its fuller identity. We don't want to linger with the trigger but instead surrender the desire to Jesus to be cultivated, to be understood, and to be released. It's easy to "see" all the time; life is visual. It takes a different mindset to actually do the work of fulfillment. Constantly seeing what others are up to can become overstimulating. Giving ourselves the freedom to step away from seeing and hearing the world can make room for allowing God to speak into what He is really trying to tell us.

In a world where connecting and social relationships continue to develop in all shapes and forms, we are called to be part of the culture. Where there are people, there is opportunity. Though we can be caught up in the negativity, we can also bring a positive force to the scene. Life is full of environments that will challenge us and also heal us if we let God into them.

In one perspective, social media can be a major drain. It can leach our freedom and our time and the relationships right in front of us, but it doesn't have to. The internet is a tool. It doesn't have to replace anything in reality, and it can be used to enhance what is true and right and good. It can be used as a means of sharing with joy, for developing relationships, and for sharing our lives and accomplishments. It is a place where we can shine, and we are meant to do so.

In its proper place, it can be a force for good. We don't have to be hindered by what we are drawn to on social media, we can be transformed into our fullness by awareness and refinement. In the midst of the business of life, we can take the time to listen to ourselves. We can make the time to listen to God.

We are here to be seen and to be enjoyed. We are here to connect and to share. We are here to give the love of God to one another. We are privileged to be able to connect with those near and far, and we can be grateful for God giving us good gifts to share and receive through the miraculous nature of technology.

So, let's be on our way! We get to live in presence and share in joy.

Day 21: Clear

Woke up today feeling great! I've exercised, drank some water, and had some quiet time before starting to get ready for school. I feel refreshed and ready to tackle my day. My mind is clear and my heart is full. I'm looking forward to going back into the social media world! I want to see my progress and see how everyone is doing.

Signing back in. Crazy enough, I had to get a new password. I didn't even remember the old one because I was always signed in.

Status Update: *How do you feel?*

"Hey Everyone! I'm back from my social media detox. I feel great! Looking forward to catching up with everybody again! See you at school!"

(20 LIKES.)

Wow! I didn't know so many people cared I was gone. That's fun.

Aww, my friend got a new puppy! Like.

What a cute shirt! Like.

The Smith's are in Europe? How awesome! Like.

Ok, well, that's probably good for now. I've got to pack my lunch and get on the bus. I'll be back to check in later, I'm sure.

All is well, social media. Life is good.

Actually, godliness is a source of profit when it is combined with being happy with what you already have.
1 Timothy 6:6

Connecting Questions: Exercise gratefulness and movement today. What are three things in your life (including social media) you can be thankful for?

Day 22: Responses

Woke up feeling great again today! I'm trying to determine how to share what I've learned from my time off. Maybe I can incorporate something at my party; I really should check and see how those invites are coming! Perhaps I can make a special toast or something.

Signing in...

(10 notifications.)

Whoa! Look at all the people who responded to my party! It looks like the other party was postponed, and people moved over to mine. It looks like everyone is really excited too; what fun responses! This will be the perfect time to celebrate the last ten days and share my detox with my friends.

"I'm so excited for all the responses to my party! I spent a lot of time with God last week, and I can't wait to see you all again face-to-face! Bring a crazy hat, and a big smile! I'll have lots of cake!"

Like. Like. Like. Like.....

This feels so good. This is what I've been hoping for but couldn't figure out how to express. I'm so glad I took the time to be away, and I can't wait for re-connecting with friends about how this party really got started!

Go, eat your food joyfully and drink happily because God has already accepted what you do.
Ecclesiastes 9:7

Connecting Questions: How can you creatively share your life? What are simple ways you can express what you are learning?

Day 23: Create

Today is the day I get to create the life I want! I was thinking it would be fun to have some sort of encouragement at my party. I want it to not only feel like a birthday celebration but also a time of connection. I want people to know that they are cared about and seen. I was thinking it could be neat to write out a bunch of prayers and put them in an empty punch bowl. Before we make a toast to officially start the party, it would be awesome to have everyone pick a piece of paper from the bowl and share the prayer they received. From there, we can toast to that! That's what my heart for my birthday is: celebration. I want our friendships to thrive and for people to feel comfortable in their own skin. I think it will be really encouraging, and my friends will love it! We all want the experience of being re-born; that's what birthdays are all about!

I should probably go back online quickly and see if I have any new responses. I'll need to know how many prayers I want to write out.

This is going to be so much fun!

I pray that your partnership in the faith might become effective by an understanding of all that is good among us in Christ.
Philemon 1:6

Connecting Questions: How can you encourage someone around you today? Who can you pray for or bless?

Day 24: Decorate

I've got the invitation going, I've got the prayers started, and I have the theme. Now it's time to get to the store and get some supplies! I'm talking about a PINATA, of course! There's no having a party without blindfolds, laughter, and candy!

I'll need to get some balloons and pick out the color theme. I'll probably be spending forever at the store, but this is full of purpose! I'm having a great time!

Looks like yellow, turquoise, and hot pink! I love it. Bags of balloons in the cart, napkins, cups, silverware, beads, streamers, and a pinata. Awesome!

(Takes a picture of the full cart of décor.)

Signing in.

Status Update: *How do you feel?*

"Guys! Look at all the fun stuff I found for the party! So excited to see you all! Let's-do-this!"

Post picture.

Like. Like. Like. Like!

Wahoo! This is so great! I've got to get home and finish planning.

Moreover, this is a gift of God: that all people should eat, drink, and enjoy the results of their hard work.
Eccelesiastes 3:13

Connecting Questions: What is your favorite way to celebrate? Plan a date to do exactly what you'd like to do.

Day 25: Excited

Four more days until the party! I can't stop thinking about how fun this has been. I've been cleaning and gathering more ideas every day. I feel so productive and so full. It's thrilling to be able to provide something from overflow instead of trying so hard to make something happen. I can't believe how taking a break from social media gave me so much more energy to be myself. There were so many things I was constantly worrying about or thinking about. My mind was so cluttered with all the drama, mental games, and mindless watching of other people's lives. This feels so much better. I feel like I have movement and grace again, like my heart is full, and my life is reflecting what I want it to reflect.

I don't know that I've ever been so excited or creative for a party! I didn't know that I would enjoy hosting so much. It was stressing me out so much before, but things have definitely shifted. The emptiness of what was is now being filled with new ideas and simple love. My brain feels like it's working the right way, and I don't even think twice about needing to be online unless I want to post what fun I've been up to. I'm having so much clarity in my life; this needs to be shared. I have joy to give away!

Signing in.

Status Update: *How do you feel?*

"GREAT. Just GREAT!"

In God we live, move, and exist.
Acts 17:28

Connecting Questions: Start a list of opportunities where you can give in your home, at your school, or in your church or community. Use your extra energy to be a force for good.

Day 26: Refreshed

I've got a lot of stuff covered for the party. I think I'll take a little break from working today and sit back and relax. I'll see what everyone has been up to.

Signing in...

I love seeing all of these status updates! It's fun having a glimpse into my friends' lives, especially those who live far away. I'm grateful that I get to be part of their lives. This is when social media feels like a real gift. I don't have to leave important friendships behind that might have never been able to continue. I love being able to see when people need something. It's nice to be able to offer a like, or an encouraging word, or a prayer. It also helps me realize when I need to set up a phone date or meet someone for coffee. It's a blessing to be aware!

It's also refreshing to be able to celebrate. I'm glad that I can see my friends living their lives; it's bringing me new joy to be able to have joy for others. It all starts from the inside. If I'm not happy and connected in my own life, I'll never be able to be celebratory for others—even my friends.

This feels like the real me. This is who I've wanted to be, and this is who I've wanted to share with my friends. I feel like I'm re-learning how to be a good friend and a person who others can trust. Integrity and joy go hand in hand.

#grateful

> **Those with sound thoughts you will keep in peace**
> **because they trust in you.**
> **Isaiah 26:3**

Connecting Questions: Take a Nap! Celebrate your new joy with new amounts of rest. Enjoy the sun. Breathe deep. Give thanks. Doodle inside the lines!

Day 27: Grateful

I'm feeling extremely grateful today. I think I need to share it with other people. My past attitude of negativity and self-hatred really didn't do well for my relationships. It didn't give me the perspective I needed to succeed, and I probably did some damage. Maybe I can at least take a small step toward reconciliation.

Signing in.

Status Update: *How do you feel?*

"Hey Everyone! I just wanted to let you know that I am really grateful for all of you, whether you live close by or far away, whether I see you often or haven't seen you in years. One thing that God taught me while being unplugged was that I have a big support system, but sometimes I have a hard time seeing it. I'm sorry if I've been a pill lately; hoping I get a do-over with some of you soon!"

Like. Like. Like.

Comments:

No worries! I get it! I need to unplug, too.

Thanks for saying this. I need to be more thankful in my life, too!

You're the best! Don't be hard on yourself; we love you. We all have bad days.

Wow. It didn't take much to make me feel better. I'm so glad I was just real. Sometimes it's easy to forget that others just need someone to start the wave, and sometimes a little vulnerability can go a long way. I feel even better. I'm so confident that this was the best way for me.

> **So then, if anyone is in Christ, that person is part of the new creation. The old things have gone away, and look, new things have arrived!**
> **2 Corinthians 5:17**

Connecting Questions: Is there anyone you need to apologize to since re-connecting with yourself? Is there anyone you can extend grace to since connecting to yourself?

Day 28: Choices

I'm determined to stay on a roll. I'm choosing the positive and releasing the negative. This feels like purpose to me!

Signing in.

Write on Erin's wall: "Erin, just wanted to let you know that I am thinking about you today. Hope you're having a great day, friend. Xoxo"

Comment on Stacy's picture: "Stacy, you look beautiful! I can't wait to see you tomorrow; it will be so great to catch up!"

Who am I jealous of? Let's get real.

Scroll.

And here I start with my "likes". I celebrate you, friend! There is room for both of us!

Signing out.

This was good. I feel like I'm making good use of my time and cleaning up a lot of messes that I may have started. Redemption feels good. Not feeling addicted to the screen feels good. Seeing friends succeed feels good. Acknowledging that there is room for everyone in every stage of their life is good. We are all unique. We are all known and loved. We all have value and worth and a life to be shared for the greater good.

This is my blood of the covenant, which is poured out for many so that their sins may be forgiven.
Matthew 26:28

Connecting Questions: Choose three people who you can encourage over social media. Find a friend who may need what you have and have what you need, and connect for collaboration.

Day 29: Party Time

PARTY DAY!! Prep is done, and I am ready. My friends are arriving any minute!

#birthday #connecting #party #dancing #laughing #encouraging #pinata #groupselfie #SELFIE

It was such a great party! I'm so grateful for all the friends who showed up. I'm so glad that I stuck it out and didn't cancel. I'm thankful that I took the time off so that I could create the party and the atmosphere that I really wanted. So many people laughed, were encouraged, met new friends, and left with full bellies. The food was tasty, everyone participated, and we all engaged with full hearts. It's as if the atmosphere I cultivated from my own heart opened up the celebration for everyone else to enter into. There was no drama; people really enjoyed themselves. I can't wait to go through my pictures and look over the new memories we've made. It's fulfilling to create true life and presence.

Tomorrow will be a great day of rest for a full labor of work. I'm going to sleep so well tonight, knowing that what God is doing in me and through me is good. There is so much redemption to create through life; I'm glad I've made the turn-around. It's only up from here.

See what kind of love the Father has given to us in that we should be called God's children, and that is what we are!
1 John 3:1

Connecting Questions: Take the time to write out what God is doing in your life with thanksgiving. Give voice to the testing and the triumph. Create a valuable story to share with others.

Day 30: Celebrate

Signing in.

Status Update: *How do you feel?*

"YOU GUYS! I am so grateful that you came to my party! I felt so loved and connected to you all. I have missed community and friendship and fun. Thank you for being part of my life; and thank you for making last night so special. I can't wait for the next get together."

Post décor pictures.
Post dancing pictures.
Post pictures of friends.
Post group selfie.
Post selfie. #beyourself #alive #me #grateful

It will be fun to see all the pictures people post. I'm looking forward to hosting again sometime. This was a good project for me in so many ways. Most importantly, I feel connected to God again. I don't feel distant or like I'm always wrestling with defeating thoughts. I know Who my source is now. He is proving Himself to me over and over again. I know the fight isn't over. There will be more to walk through, more to contemplate, and more to release in surrender. One party doesn't redeem it all, but it surely is a start. Thank you for the tool belt, God. Thank you for the silence and for the connection. Thank you for revealing Yourself to me when I was honest and allowed myself the room for my thoughts. Thank you for showing up for me in the middle of my mess. Thank you for wiping away my tears, even in the girls' bathroom. I'm so grateful for You; I'm so glad I'm me. I'm glad to be here. I love my new selfie.

> ***Instead, we are God's accomplishment, created in Christ Jesus to do good things. God planned for these good things to be the way that we live our lives.***
> ***Ephesians 2:10***

Connecting Questions: Create a short mission statement for your life. You have a life to live and places to go! What did you learn about who you are and what you love? How can this be simply honored in your daily life?

The Breakdown

The Negative Side:

Wasting Time: How many hours of the day does social media take up in your life? How much time do you get to spend outdoors or socially engaging with others around you? How does mindless "entertainment" really make you feel?

A Comparison Magnet:
How often do you look at social media and compare your life to what others are doing? Do you often receive the pressure to perform instead of having the peace of presence?

Addiction to Drama:
Social media can foster gossip, jealousy, and eavesdropping. How are you when it comes to engaging arguments, judgements, and controversy online? Are you able to express emotions in a healthy way?

Crippling Self-Esteem:
Are you overwhelmed and un-started on projects you'd like to do? Does screen time encourage procrastination in your life? Overuse of technology can cause depression and anxiety to surface; how do you create boundaries with the screen in your life?
When only connected online and not face to face, do friendships seem less "essential" or less of a priority to you?
Who are your "real" friends? What is your "real" life like?
Do you feel seen and valued outside of the social media world?

The Messy Middle:

What are your online triggers?
What does that reveal about your needs?
What is the best way to connect with God in order to fulfill these needs?
What are healthy boundaries that need to be made in order to foster personal growth?
What is your NEW STORY to share with the world?

The Positive Side:

Learn Time Management, Priorities:
How do you manage priorities first so that social media is a reflection of your time well spent?

Share your tips with others on how you've done so!
Let your new healthy boundaries encourage discipline and favor in your life!

Make the Time to Create Your Life:
Find ways to express yourself and your life online creatively through photos, writing, or music (You just may find a new hobby!)
Engage your friends in these activities.
Fuel your brain by doing instead of waiting to be entertained; creativity is refreshing.

Enjoy Relationships!
Especially those who don't live by you.
Pray for one another, "be" with one another in loss and in celebration.
Share ideas, memories, and holidays.
Express gratitude.
Share funny and real life stories.
Be authentic in a world of that is drowning in shallow waters.

Contribute! Be a Light!
Contribute to positive conversations with your input; create positive conversations.
Share what you've learned from your connection with God.
Post articles and thoughts that share wisdom and offer solutions.
Share ideas, support others with your strengths.

Butterflies & Blooms:

A Creative Devo for Tweens & Teens

Sarah Humphrey

Intro:

Weighed down by the expectations and demands of performance and perfectionism, it can be exhausting and difficult to fit into the tightly-knit boxes that have been shaped for females and personalities of all sizes. What we see in magazines and on book covers gives us the glimpse into what we seemingly "should" aspire to be, but sadly the airbrushed and edited images don't leave much room for the processing of real feelings, the guidance for true answers, and the space to find ourselves without getting into trouble. Young women want to be known, to be understood, and to belong. That's God's nature to all of us actually, from baby to granny. We are feelers, and creators, and yet we need security to bloom. Where we look for the validation to life's most basic needs can have profound effects on how our hearts beat, what our future looks like, and if our dreams become reality. While every girl may not want to live as a fairytale, every girl desires to be loved. It's in our DNA because we are His Beloved.

Topics like identity, shame, fear, grief, intimacy, and self-acceptance are key holders during the formative years of learning about womanhood. All of these themes can be wrestled with in prayer. When we talk to God, we transform our reality. He has given us everything we need inside of us as His spirit lives in us.

Through this 30 day journey, I hope your passion for God's presence is made real in new ways. I hope you find safety and peace in belonging to the heart of God. I pray you find good opportunities to search out your dreams and goals. I believe you will discover new things about yourself as you process through these pages--and as you add color to your already blooming, beautiful life.

Enjoy the journey!

Sarah

Table of Contents:

Live Simply.

The world will tell you to buy more, be more, do more...

I have come to tell you the opposite. What I once thought was staying hip to the trends, I have now come to find out is not worth it. Busy is not necessarily better. Hustle is not always the answer. Is there space for movement? Absolutely. It's easy to get depressed if we don't keep moving, but we can get overwhelmed if we carry too much. My only solution to this high-tech and fast-paced life is learning how to be present, living simply, and then giving practically. This has brought me joy, peace, and progress. It's easy to be distracted by phones, and media, and movies. Don't let your life be easy. Let your life be creative! In order to create well, it's important to be still. Become yourself! Know who you are because of Whose you are. Take the time to squish the possibilities of anxiety by minimizing your materials and schedule so that you can maximize your life and your gifts.

You won't regret it. Start small and authentic. Choose what you really love, and let the extra fall away.

Our first 5 days together are about living simply. See you inside!

Day 1:

Before I start a creative process, I love a clean room. I love to de-clutter and freshen up my space in order to feel like there is order in my heart. It gives me the balance and the strength I need to dig deep with God and to get cozy in my surroundings. There is beauty in simplicity; it's nice to know that when I have big feelings to work through, I can have a clear space to create. Before we ever fly, we bloom. And before we bloom, we pray. And to be honest, before I pray-- I clean. It just seems to help me flow.

Take 10 minutes today to clear up some clutter in your room. What are a few things you can get rid of that you don't need? Any pieces of trash hanging around? Any cobwebs in the corners? It feels good to get rid of what is no longer needed and what no longer helps us.

Meditate here:
Create a clean heart for me, God; Put a new, faithful spirit deep inside me!
Psalm 51:10

_____

_____

_____

_____

_____

Day 2:

A clean room sets the stage for prayer. Cozy up with a hot drink and a blanket, find a quiet place to sit, and ask God to show Himself to you. Sometimes it's in these simple, small moments that God can speak to us most clearly. When we purposefully quiet ourselves, give Him room to speak, and set our heart to listening, we can engage in His desires for us. It's simple. Stop and listen; He has good plans for you! Share your feelings; He cares about the details. Allow Him to give you peace and joy in the conversation. There's no better place to refresh than to have a "coffee" date with God.

Meditate here:

Be still and know that I am God!
Psalm 46:10

Day 3:

Sometimes we need some sunshine or a flower to inspire us with the beauty of God's creation. Find some nature to enjoy today. If it's nice, take a walk with a friend. If it's cold, sit on the porch for a few minutes. If it's hot, take a dip at the local pool or park. We need God's creation in a world of computers and phones. It's good to take the time to enjoy a few minutes to breathe fresh air, to nourish our souls with nature, and to live in the beauty that God designed Himself.

What are some of your favorite ways to enjoy the outdoors? How does God speak to you through nature? What is your favorite season of the year and why?

Meditate here:
His coming is as brilliant as the sunrise.
Habakkuk 3:4

_____
_____
_____
_____
_____

Day 4:

Time-wasters can create chaos in our lives. They can slow down our productivity, keep us from doing what is needed, and they can make us stay in a cycle of defeat. When we can focus on a goal or a practical exercise, it's good for our souls. When we get easily distracted by too much noise or too many activities or even too much schoolwork, we can start to lose ourselves. Learning how to manage time keeps us joyful in the long run. If we want to chase our hopes and dreams, we'll need to learn how to limit the excess of what hinders our progress. What is your favorite way to feel alive? What are some of the needed chores that are required of you? How can you focus on what needs to be done so that you can make room for what makes your heart beat?

Meditate here:
Look straight ahead. Fix your eyes on what lies before you.
Proverbs 4:25

_____
_____
_____
_____
_____

Day 5:

Before we get moving, it's always good to stretch. It's what you do before exercise to make sure there isn't an injury; it's also what you do when you want to expand your knowledge in ways that will make you grow. Take a few minutes today to bring your body into alignment. Give yourself the room to stretch to some of your favorite music, take deep breaths, and watch as your body relaxes and becomes ready for transition. When growing in a cocoon, a caterpillar pushes against the sides and stretches as it matures. During this stage of transformation, we do the same. Without being challenged, we won't bloom. And without blooming, we won't fly. There's always a series of steps, each one taking enough time to encourage the next one. Give yourself some time to breathe today, stretch your body, and be ready to exercise your creativity!

Meditate here:

But grow in the grace and knowledge of our Lord and Savior Jesus Christ.
To him be glory both now and forever! Amen.
2 Peter 3:18

_____

_____

_____

_____

_____

Identify YOU and Your Dreams.

There is an innate desire within a young woman to know who she is, where she belongs, and how she can contribute to the world in a way that is beautiful. Our identity is first shaped by the voices who speak to us, the prayers spoken over us, and the environment we are birthed into. What we all long for is belonging, peace, and joy. We chase hopes, and we dream dreams in an attempt to capture how our heart beats, because within those beats is the presence of our Creator. In the womb of our mother, we listen for the sound that has given us a name. Our greatest calling is to receive the love that we were created for in its many forms and journeys, so that we can continue to give to others exponentially. Exploring those roads leads to destination, and destination always finds its home in Him. So, dream another dream, and hope another hope. Let's find ourselves in the heartbeat of the One who loves us most!

Day 6:

It's amazing how our lives are shaped by our names. Everyone uses our names to call for us, to speak to us, or to identify us. It is the primary way for how we are known. If we look into what we are called, we can find answers to our identity and to our personal story. It's in our name that we are recognized. What is your name? What does it mean? Why did your parents give you your particular name? Do you like your name or not like it? Find out who you are by studying what you've been called.

Meditate here:

Do not fear, for I have redeemed you; I have summoned you by name. You are mine.
Isaiah 43:1

Day 7:

Everything we do carries energy, either positive or negative. Sometimes it's easy to get character confused with performance. Who you are is what you carry with you: Love, Joy, Peace, Patience, Kindness, Goodness, Faithfulness, Gentleness, and Self-control. What do you most want to "be"? And why? What do you most want to exemplify from the inside out?

Meditate here:

But the fruit of the Spirit is love, joy, peace, forbearance, kindness, goodness, faithfulness, gentleness, and self-control. Against such things there is no law.
Galatians 5:22-23

Day 8:

What we do comes from who we are. If we carry the fruit of the Spirit with us wherever we go, we will always have an opportunity to serve with our gifts and talents. What would you most like to do? What are your particular gifts and talents? How do you share who you are with others? What we like to do shows us how we can give to the world around us. Our gifts are like a tool belt, and the fruit of the Spirit is the power source. If we have the mind of Christ and are seasoned with the Spirit, we can offer our gifts to be used by God to touch other people.

Meditate here:

God has given each of you a gift. Use it to help each other. This will show God's loving-favor.

I Peter 4:10-11

_____

_____

_____

_____

_____

Day 9:

Our strengths are the places within us that God has already developed or where we naturally are gifted. It's important to know where we feel confident and strong because it shows us how we can teach those around us. When we share our strengths, we extend love and care for someone. What are your strengths? What do you feel you do well? How do these translate from you as a person and also as a friend?

Mediate here:

Let us help each other to love others and to do good.
Hebrews 10:24

_____
_____
_____
_____
_____

Day 10:

It's just as important to know where we are weak as well as where we are strong. When we are weak in an area, it just means that we need to gain authority in our situation. Authority is simply a synonym for a person who has overcome a struggle. When we learn how to overcome, it teaches us humility, how to ask for help, and how to receive. What are your current weaknesses? Where would you like to grow in authority?

It's important to remember that everything in our identity is designed for love! God loves us, and He created us for connection and for a purpose. We can do both when we lean into His heart for us, receive grace from Him, and listen to truth from the Scriptures. Sometimes in our weakness, it helps to find a favorite story from the Bible that resembles our situation. Can you discover a person in the Bible who may have the same strengths/weaknesses as you? What can you learn from him/her?

Meditate here:
Let His banner over me be love.
Song of Songs 2:4

_____
_____
_____
_____
_____

Fear Transforms into Faith.

Fear is too often a companion for girls. It slithers its way into our hearts to convince us to believe lies about our worth, our beauty, and our goodness. When God made us, He said "It is good." He loves us with a perfect and unconditional love. Because our world system is broken and in need of healing, we don't want to listen to who the world says females are. We want to understand who God has made us to be. Even if we are broken in spirit, God says that "He is close to those who are crushed in spirit, and He binds up the brokenhearted (Psalm 34:18)". Jesus is a safe person for us to express our fear and feelings with. He is not ashamed of emotions, and He can connect with us best as we release our honest thoughts to Him while asking Him to guide us to a healed and whole version of ourselves. Let's express some of our fears on paper. When we name what scares us, it starts to lose its power. Use the blank space below to write down a few of your fears. We'll use the next few days to ask God to transform these fears into faith.

Day 11:

If we talk about fear, we have to talk about comparison. Comparison is a killer of happiness, peace, and joy. When we see something we like (or don't like) in another person, it's often our first cue to connect with ourselves. We can have the life we desire! Usually, if we are in a cycle of comparison, we simply just need to learn how to cultivate who we are. Make a list of a few things that you admire in others that you'd like to cultivate in yourself with God's help. Then use the space below to write down what might make you jealous. Ask God how you can connect with Him and yourself to transform you into who you'd like to be. Usually what makes us jealous, is actually what we are most called to redeem through our own story! We have authority over jealousy and comparison when we have experienced our acceptance in Christ. You are worthy of love and connection; let God help you grow your desires within you!

Meditate here:

Let the morning bring me word of your unfailing love, for I have put my trust in you.
Psalm 143:8-9

Day 12:

Believing we are unworthy of something is a trigger to a poverty mindset, which leads to a road of hopelessness. God wouldn't make someone He didn't love. God loves to lavish us with gifts. He also holds those gifts for the appropriate time because of His wisdom for our well-being. We are worth love and connection and giftedness; sometimes we just need to be cleared of self-rejection first so we can accept God's gift fully! What are some of your desires? Find some Scriptures that speak into these desires. They will give you wisdom while you wait for God's timing.

Meditate here:

But you are a chosen people, a royal priesthood, a holy nation, God's special possession, that you may declare the praises of him who called you out of darkness into his wonderful light.

1 Peter 2:9

_____

_____

_____

_____

_____

Day 13:

Shame often hinders us from sharing our true selves. When we ask ourself questions like "What will people think?" or "Who am I to do something awesome like that?", we diminish our own value. When we think we are not enough, we've believed a lie. Shame tries to cover our God-given gifts illegally. We can look at God with an honest face because with Him, we are never ashamed. If we need to repent of a bad decision, we can repent. But we never have to feel condemned. What are some of your repetitive, negative thought patterns? What are the opposite of those patterns? Focus your attention on the positive!

Meditate here:

Those who look to Him are radiant; their faces are never covered in shame.
Psalm 34:5

Day 14:

Rejection plays a crucial part in fear's tactics because the places where we've once been hurt can open up again when we try something new or creative. In every woman's life, there has been rejection of some sort. This is because we live in a broken world and because our greatest calling is to be loved and to show love. For every beautiful intention of God, there is an opposite counterfeit. Sometimes we learn how to reject ourselves because others haven't been able to see who we are and have hurt us. Write down some situations in your life where people may have hurt your feelings. After releasing them onto paper, ask God to start to fill your heart with acceptance and peace. This is the key step before forgiveness can start to take place.

Meditate here:

You are my hiding place; you will protect me from trouble and surround me with songs of deliverance. Psalm 32:7

_____

_____

_____

_____

_____

Day 15:

Sometimes we are just as scared of our own calling as we are of what other people may think about us. Fear blows a smoke screen over our real identity, and its goal is to keep us shut down. When we replace fear with faith, we become more confident and accept ourselves much more. Look back to the beginning of this section at the fears you wrote down. What are the opposites of those fears? Also, what is something you might be scared to do but you also really want to do? Is there a small step you can take to start moving toward your dreams and away from your fears?

Meditate here:

Now faith is confidence in what we hope for and assurance about what we do not see.
Hebrews 11:1

_____

_____

_____

_____

_____

Intimacy with God.

Women were created for emotional intimacy and connection. What we receive from God can be given to others as a gift. We can nurture, support, and care for others as we receive God's love and care for ourselves. The level of emotional connection filters to a physical connection as we grow in age and explore marriage and sexuality. It's always in our best interests to grow intimate from the inside out. God puts boundaries on our sexuality within marriage because it is what makes us most vulnerable to love or to heartbreak. Before giving yourself to anyone else, it's most satisfying to be in connection to God first. This gives love and intimacy it's proper outlet in our lives.

Day 16:

One of the best ways to emotionally connect is to rewrite our stories and rewire the parts of our thinking that have been broken or damaged. Handwriting rewires our limbic system (which is our brain's center for reason, logic, and emotions). When we write the Truth, we carve new pathways in our minds to actually believe it. Some of us may have had a difficult past, but we can allow God to reconnect us, reshape us, and reform us as we put our thoughts onto paper. Where would you like a do-over? What would you like to write or re-write?

Meditate here:

I will put my law in their minds and write it on their hearts.
I will be their God, and they will be my people.
Jeremiah 31:33

_____
_____
_____
_____
_____

Day 17:

We are often held back from intimacy and connection when we haven't had an opportunity to grieve. The world often says "Turn that frown upside down!" or asks us to put on a fake face in order to impress, perform, or survive. When we allow ourselves to work through genuine seasons of sadness, we can release stored grief that is keeping us from our potential. It's helpful to go through our emotions and not around them. Journaling is a great outlet for allowing stuffed emotions to flow. Simply write how you feel. Use the space below to put down some of your thoughts and feelings on paper. You can be completely honest here!

Meditate here:

There is a time for everything, and a season for every activity under the heavens.
Ecclesiastes 3:1

Day 18:

Sometimes we want connection or company so badly that it can be easy to overextend ourselves into outside activity. The times we most need to rest and process can often be sidetracked by busyness and extracurricular activities. Constant motion without time to catch up with our hearts can lead to exhaustion and burn out. Our lives are supposed to be fun and full of activity and replenishment! What are a few ways you can connect with yourself today? They can be as simple as praying, creating art, reading a favorite book, or organizing your room.

Meditate here:

He will cover you with His feathers and under His wings you will find refuge; His faithfulness will be your shield and your rampart.
Psalm 91:4

_____

_____

_____

_____

_____

Day 19:

Close friendships can support us by giving us a connection for fun, teamwork, and growth. It's important to choose friends who can encourage us to be the best versions of ourselves. When we pick friends who make us feel like we have to measure up to be accepted, who gives us advice that isn't rooted in purity, and who don't create a safe environment for us to share our God-given talents, it might be time to reconsider if these relationships are a good idea. Making a boundary to maintain friendships that foster creativity, joy, and balance is a great way to create long-sustaining relationships.

Who are your best friends? What relationships create compromise? Pray about how to grow with integrity.

Meditate here:

As iron sharpens iron, so a friend sharpens a friend.
Proverbs 27:17

_____

_____

_____

_____

_____

Day 20:

Choosing to be vulnerable in a relationship by sharing your heart can be a big gift in friendship. Being able to share your true feelings with someone when you need help is a key to moving forward during difficult emotions or situations. Asking God for wisdom about who and what to share is equally important. If you've surrounded yourself with people who have had a positive influence on you, you'll be much more safe to share your heart. If you've had a hard time with friendships and aren't sure where to go, finding an adult or youth leader that you trust is a good idea. Create a "safe" list of your closest and most beneficial friendships and mentor relationships. This is always good to go back to when you might need help or counsel.

Meditate here:

Listen to advice and accept discipline; and at the end you will be counted among the wise.
Proverbs 19:20

_____
_____
_____
_____
_____

Be Kind To Yourself.

What makes a young woman most confident is when she lives unashamedly as herself. Self-esteem comes from self-acceptance, the gentle and kind comfort we give to all our weak spots, sad memories, and sacred spaces in our hearts and minds. No one comes to this planet with a perfect life; there have been generational lines of blessings and mistakes that have shaped our environment and our minds. What we learn in self-acceptance is peace. What God most wants us to know is that He understands us more than we do, and He loves us with every breath. He doesn't try to fix us; He simply wants to be with us, in every single hurt and in every single joy.

Day 21:

Reminding ourselves of our identity in Christ is a gateway to self-acceptance. He is inside us, and as we abide in Him, we allow Him to give us wings. Google "Bible verses on identity in Christ". See what verses ring the most true for you, and write down a few below--including your mediation verse. Place these verses on a notecard and post them where you can see them regularly. You can even add one to the blank space in the coloring page at the end of this section. Turn a few pages to find it!

Meditate here:

I praise you because I am fearfully and wonderfully made;
your works are wonderful, I know that full well.
Psalm 139:14

Day 22:

Boundaries are a great way to give our freedom the safest place to bloom. When we accept ourselves, we often want to help others understand their worth as well. The context of how we do that is so important in order for our generosity to be stewarded in a healthy way. It's essential to know your value, so you know where to create boundaries for your well-being.

Where can you currently say yes to serving in a safe and productive way? Where do you need to say no to serving for the time being? If you are in between yes and no? Then pray.

Meditate here:

Do not forsake wisdom, and she will protect you; love her, and she will watch over you.
Proverbs 4:6

_____

_____

_____

_____

_____

Day 23:

Failure happens. In this life, there are mistakes, and heartache, and blunders. We may try, and we may fail. People may not understand us. People may judge us. But when we move toward the God in us, which is a reflection of our true self, we can always learn through failure. This is the normal process of life, and even failure can turn into one of our greatest teaching tools if we learn from every experience we go through. Mistakes can end up being helpful; they teach us how to improve and grow.

What are some of your mistakes? What can you learn from them?

Meditate here:

My grace is sufficient for you, for my power is made perfect in weakness.
2 Corinthians 12:9

_____

_____

_____

_____

_____

Day 24:

Grace is free! Jesus loves us no matter what. A steadfast heart and an honest journey gives us the keys to understanding God's free gift to us. We don't have to be perfect; we just have to be willing to listen to wisdom, read the Bible, and be open to adventure. Take some time to write down some of the ways God has shown you grace through your gifts and through your mistakes. He makes everything clean!

Meditate here:

Love never fails.
I Corinthians 13:8

Day 25:

Love is unconditional. Relationships on Earth can fail us or end, but God never leaves us nor denies us of His love. He is ever-present as we learn how to gently love ourselves and love others. He is consistent, kind, and always with us. What are some of your favorite ways to spend time with God? Write them down. Make sure to give yourself extra time in your life just to be with Him and enjoy His presence and love.

Meditate here.

My presence shall go with you, and I will give you rest.
Exodus 33:14

_____
_____
_____
_____
_____

Our Life
As a
Creative Prayer.

Everything we need comes from our Father. He has provided everything for us to live an adventurous, beautiful, and fun-filled life in Him. Even when we might feel lonely, sad, or confused, He will satisfy our hearts. In Him, all dreams come true. We find purpose for our gifts when we understand His will is simply friendship with Him.

Day 26:

Gratitude fosters a healthy outlook on life. When we complain or grumble, we miss out on blessing. When we are thankful and look for reasons to be happy, we find that more and more gifts open to us. We can be grateful in any situation, even when we don't understand it, because He has proven to us that He is unconditional and full of love. He loves even when we can't see it. Write down some of the things you are grateful for below, big and small!

Meditate here:

Give thanks in all circumstances; for this is God's will for you in Christ Jesus.
1 Thessalonians 5:18

_____

_____

_____

_____

_____

Day 27:

Hope is the result of gratitude. As we see opportunities arrive because we have stewarded gratefulness in our hearts, we see hopelessness flee and our dreams come true. When we have our Hope set on Him, anything is possible. What are some of the things you hope for? You can move toward what you hope for in the natural as you hope in Him, and He shows you the way.

Meditate here:

"For I know the plans I have for you," declares the LORD, "plans to prosper you and not to harm you, plans to give you hope and a future."
Jeremiah 29:11

_____

_____

_____

_____

_____

Day 28:

Forgiveness is made easy when we have been grateful for our current life and have hope for the future. When we live from a full well, it's easier to give grace to others who have hurt us. We can live in a place of generosity toward others when we have been present with God. He is always forgiving and always wise. He forgives us so that we can be free. We forgive in order to untangle ourselves and others. Even when the forgiveness we give isn't given back, we don't have to live with guilt or old wounds. We are responsible for our actions and should apologize whenever necessary. We also should forgive as we are able. Sometimes it's a long process of feelings and work, and that's ok if we keep moving forward until we are free. Grace has been given to us, and we can set healthy boundaries to give us security for the future. Forgiveness is the best place to live. Trust must be earned again, but giving grace sets us up for personal success. Who might you need to forgive? Why? Acknowledge why the circumstance hurt. Ask God to be with you as you learn how to let it go.

Meditate here:

In Him we have redemption through his blood, the forgiveness of sins,
in accordance with the riches of God's grace.
Ephesians 1:7

Day 29:

We can live a splendidly, imperfect life by living a life of prayer. Gratitude leads to hope, and hope leads to forgiveness. Forgiveness allows us to apologize for where we've gone wrong and to change our actions for the future. It also allows us to heal from those who have hurt us and helps us set healthy boundaries. As we learn Whose we are, we learn who we are. And everything in between is prayer. From the smallest detail to the greatest achievement, our identity is birthed in Him and for Him. As we pray our life's prayer, we learn purpose and grace and belonging. We live splendidly, imperfect lives as we accept where we are and move toward where we want to be. We move through metamorphosis into blooming beauty as we become fully present with our Creator. Write some of your prayer requests below, for yourself and for others. Start to pray!

Meditate here:

I pray that your hearts will be flooded with light so that you can understand the confident hope he has given to those he called—his holy people who are his rich and glorious inheritance.

Ephesians 1:18

_____

_____

_____

_____

_____

Day 30:

Growing into womanhood can be messy, and it can be fun. There isn't one formula, but there is wisdom in healthy boundaries. There can be a lot of color, and freedom, and expression in our paths as we navigate our emotions, our dreams, and our hearts. With each step into God and into ourselves, we can see His nature grow in us as we embody beauty spiritually and naturally. It is a gift to be female. We get to express the nature of God that shows nurture, compassion, and strength. Sometimes the road can be difficult, but God always provides a good outlet of expression for us. He is good, and He loves us just the way we are. When we come to Him with our hearts, He will never fail us! Live beautifully. Live freely. Forgive, love, and seek wisdom. Fly high, butterflies!

Meditate here:

Live freely, animated and motivated by God's Spirit.
Galatians 5:16

Be YOU.

30 practical prayers for living in your God-given design

Sarah Humphrey

Table of Contents:

~~~

Prayer helps us stay in tune with God, keeps us grounded, and makes life exciting! Growing through the teen years can be full of fun, choices, and preparation. These 30 blessings are designed as a quick way to guide you into God's heart every day. Divided into ten topics, you can be blessed in identity, growth, passion, motives, expression, friendship, giving, rest, movement, and prayer here!

~~~

Who am I?

Identify your strengths.

Peace

I call my spirit forward in the name of Jesus, to be honored and to be blessed. Scriptures say that your peace passes all understanding, and so I bless myself to receive that peace within my deepest turmoil.

May my heart not fret but know your Hand. May my spirit seek wisdom, and may patience be rooted within me. May I trust your love, your plan, and your grace. May I give you my fear in exchange for your protection. May courage rise up where my life has been hindered. May strength fill me where I've been weakened by battle.

May my soul rest under the faith of my spirit. May my body connect where trauma once was. May I be blessed with peace in my innermost being.

I ask for alignment in all these things. May God, Jesus, and the Holy Spirit fill and align me spirit, soul, and body today. May I receive revelation from your Voice and confirmation in your Word. May my mouth always praise You.

Philippians 4:4-9

Be glad in the Lord always! Again, I say, be glad! Let your gentleness show in your treatment of all people. The Lord is near. Don't be anxious about anything; rather, bring up all of your requests to God in your prayers and petitions, along with giving of thanks. Then the peace of God that exceeds all understanding will keep your hearts and minds safe in Christ Jesus. From now on, brothers and sisters, if anything is excellent and if anything is admirable, focus your thoughts on these things: all that is true, all that is holy, all that is just, all that is pure, all that is lovely, all that is worthy of praise. Practice these things: whatever you learned, received, heard, or saw in us. The God of peace will be with you.

Joy

I call my spirit forward in the name of Jesus, to be blessed and to be honored. The Scriptures say let everything that has breath praise the Lord, and so I bless myself with joy.

In the deepest sense of longsuffering comes the greatest sense of joy. May I learn how to offer my struggles and my shame daily, remembering that your burden is easy and your yoke is light. May I see from the perspective of depth instead of from the quick fix of immediate gratification. May my faith rise as I lean into your presence, knowing that as you are the highest choice, I can always be filled with hope.

May my soul be healed in the most broken of parts. May portions in darkness receive your light. May my mind rest under the leading of my spirit. May my body be filled to overflowing under the joy of my spirit and soul.

I ask for alignment in all these things. May God, Jesus, and the Holy Spirit fill and align me spirit, soul, and body today. May I receive revelation from your Voice and confirmation in your Word. May my mouth always praise You.

Psalm 150

Praise the Lord.

Praise God in his sanctuary;

praise him in his mighty heavens.

Praise him for his acts of power;

praise him for his surpassing greatness.

Praise him with the sounding of the trumpet,

praise him with the harp and lyre,

praise him with timbrel and dancing,

praise him with the strings and pipe,

praise him with the clash of cymbals,

praise him with resounding cymbals.

Let everything that has breath praise the Lord.

Praise the Lord.

Revealed

I call my spirit forward in the name of Jesus, to be blessed and to be honored. The Scriptures say that you have revealed your righteousness to the Nations, and so I bless myself with sight. It is your work on the cross that saves us in all ways abundantly. You make known who you are and what you have graciously done for us.

May my spirit be filled with the fear of the Lord, the grace of your heart, and the agreement of my will. May I experience your heart for me as I put all my faith in you. May my mind be consecrated to your plan and your path. May my soul grow in mindful work, obedience, and prayer. May I trust in your leadership and be fruitful through my body.

I ask for alignment in all these things. May God, Jesus, and the Holy Spirit fill and align me spirit, soul, and body today. May I receive revelation from your Voice and confirmation in your Word. May my mouth always praise You.

Psalm 98:2

The Lord has made known his salvation;
he has revealed his righteousness in the sight of the nations.

Where can I grow?

Identify your weak spots.

K n o w n

I call my spirit forward in the name of Jesus, to be honored and to be blessed. The Scriptures say every hair on my head is numbered, that you keep record of all my days, and so I bless myself with identity.

May I be blessed with a deep and profound understanding that you know my heart and every need before I speak it. May I be blessed with the abundance of your presence, knowing you plan for my best, and prepare me for it during my days. May the hidden chores of my day be an offering to you, and may my sacrifices be of great worth toward restoration on Earth.

May my soul rest under the shadow of my filled and quiet spirit. May it breathe in peace and legitimacy, expressing that you are all-seeing and all-knowing. May my body receive fulfillment in my bones, as it moves and has its being in you.

I ask for alignment in all these things. May God, Jesus, and the Holy Spirit fill and align me spirit, soul, and body today. May I receive revelation from your Voice and confirmation in your Word. May my mouth always praise You.

Psalm 139

Lord, you have examined me.
You know me.
You know when I sit down and when I stand up.
Even from far away, you comprehend my plans.
You study my traveling and resting.
You are thoroughly familiar with all my ways.
There isn't a word on my tongue, Lord,
that you don't already know completely.
You surround me—front and back.
You put your hand on me.
That kind of knowledge is too much for me;
it's so high above me that I can't fathom it.
Where could I go to get away from your spirit?
Where could I go to escape your presence?
If I went up to heaven, you would be there.
If I went down to the grave, you would be there too!
If I could fly on the wings of dawn,
stopping to rest only on the far side of the ocean—

even there your hand would guide me;
even there your strong hand would hold me tight!
If I said, "The darkness will definitely hide me;
the light will become night around me,"
even then the darkness isn't too dark for you!
Nighttime would shine bright as day,
because darkness is the same as light to you!
You are the one who created my innermost parts;
you knit me together while I was still in my mother's womb.
I give thanks to you that I was marvelously set apart.
Your works are wonderful—I know that very well.
My bones weren't hidden from you
when I was being put together in a secret place,
when I was being woven together in the deep parts of the earth.
Your eyes saw my embryo,
and on your scroll every day was written that was being formed for me,
before any one of them had yet happened.
God, your plans are incomprehensible to me!
Their total number is countless!
If I tried to count them—they outnumber grains of sand!
If I came to the very end—I'd still be with you.

Accepted

I call my spirit forward in the name of Jesus, to be blessed and to be honored. The Scriptures say I am fully accepted into the heart of the Father, and so I bless myself with belonging.

Within each day, let my heart know acceptance. May my spirit comprehend the fruitfulness and the complete satisfaction of God. May I align to be loved, to be valued, and to be lead.

May my soul come into submission to love. May my mind be available for self-control, long-suffering, and peace. In my thoughts, may I be willing to yield to holiness as it makes its way in me. May my body resonate with gladness, fully open to its best care and available for movements of grace.

I ask for alignment in all these things. May God, Jesus, and the Holy Spirit fill and align me spirit, soul, and body today. May I receive revelation from your Voice and confirmation in your Word. May my mouth always praise You.

Ephesians 1:3-13

Bless the God and Father of our Lord Jesus Christ! He has blessed us in Christ with every spiritual blessing that comes from heaven. God chose us in Christ to be holy and blameless in God's presence before the creation of the world. God destined us to be his adopted children through Jesus Christ because of his love. This was according to his goodwill and plan and to honor his glorious grace that he has given to us freely through the Son whom he loves. We have been ransomed through his Son's blood, and we have forgiveness for our failures based on his overflowing grace, which he poured over us with wisdom and understanding. God revealed his hidden design to us, which is according to his goodwill and the plan that he intended to accomplish through his Son. This is what God planned for the climax of all times: to bring all things together in Christ, the things in heaven along with the things on earth. We have also received an inheritance in Christ. We were destined by the plan of God, who accomplishes everything according to his design. We are called to be an honor to God's glory because we were the first to hope in Christ. You too heard the word of truth in Christ, which is the good news of your salvation. You were sealed with the promised Holy Spirit because you believed in Christ.

Creative

I call my spirit forward in the name of Jesus, to be blessed and to be honored. Jesus said "Let the little children come to me; for theirs is the Kingdom of Heaven", and so I bless myself with creativity.

May my spirit remember the nature of childlike faith. May I take delight in His redemption through me. May I be free to explore, play, and create. May the Holy Spirit lead me into the restoration of my inherent gifts. As my spirit fills with purity, may my soul rest with joy. As my mind is renewed with hope and laughter, let my body be exalted into your healing and grace.

I ask for alignment in all these things. May God, Jesus, and the Holy Spirit fill and align me spirit, soul, and body today. May I receive revelation from your Voice and confirmation in your Word. May my mouth always praise You.

Matthew 19:13-15

Some people brought children to Jesus so that he would place his hands on them and pray. But the disciples scolded them. "Allow the children to come to me," Jesus said. "Don't forbid them, because the kingdom of heaven belongs to people like these children." Then he blessed the children and went away from there.

What do I love to do?

Identify your passion.

Delighted

I call my spirit forward in the name of Jesus, to be honored and to be blessed. The Scriptures say you sing songs of deliverance over me, and you rejoice over me with singing. Not only do you care about me, but you also delight in me. And so I bless myself with adoration.

May my spirit completely cultivate an understanding of delight. May I rest in the guidance and trust of your good will toward me. May my soul heal from all the places I've been wounded, neglected, or abused. May stillness be birthed where fear once lived. May my body exalt a sound mind, moving with grace, power and purity, manifested from a spirit who embraces belonging in the Son.

I ask for alignment in all these things. May God, Jesus, and the Holy Spirit fill and align me spirit, soul, and body today. May I receive revelation from your Voice and confirmation in your Word. May my mouth always praise You.

Zephaniah 3:17

Rejoice, Daughter Zion! Shout, Israel!
Rejoice and exult with all your heart, Daughter Jerusalem.
The Lord has removed your judgment;
he has turned away your enemy.
The Lord, the king of Israel, is in your midst;
you will no longer fear evil.
On that day, it will be said to Jerusalem:
Don't fear, Zion.
Don't let your hands fall.
The Lord your God is in your midst—a warrior bringing victory.
He will create calm with his love;
he will rejoice over you with singing.
I will remove from you those worried about the appointed feasts.
They have been a burden for her, a reproach.
Watch what I am about to do to all your oppressors at that time.
I will deliver the lame;
I will gather the outcast.
I will change their shame into praise and fame throughout the earth.
At that time, I will bring all of you back,
at the time when I gather you.
I will give you fame and praise among all the neighboring peoples
when I restore your possessions and you can see them—says the Lord.

Fulfilled

I call my spirit forward in the name of Jesus, to be blessed and to be honored. The Scriptures say that the word you send out of your mouth will not return void, so I bless myself with fulfillment. It is in communion with you that we grow, are satisfied, are strengthened, and are radiant as children of God.

May my spirit be filled with joy, fullness, and overflowing grace. May I experience your heart and your works in all ways that lead to mission and purpose. May my mind be girded with the spirit and the truth. May my soul be refreshed by the grace of Your hand. May my body flourish as I finish the assignments you've divinely assigned to me.

I ask for alignment in all these things. May God, Jesus, and the Holy Spirit fill and align me spirit, soul, and body today. May I receive revelation from your Voice and confirmation in your Word. May my mouth always praise You.

Isaiah 55:11

So shall my word be that goes out from my mouth;

it shall not return to me empty,

but it shall accomplish that which I purpose,

and shall succeed in the thing for which I sent it.

Self-Control

I call my spirit forward in the name of Jesus, to be blessed and to be honored. The Scriptures say that self-control is one of the fruits of the Spirit, and so I bless myself with wisdom and peace.

May my spirit be enriched with the hand that teaches me and shows me kindness through authority. May I heed warning and stay within healthy boundaries in all areas of life. May my soul be refreshed by obedience in God, and may it also relish in protection through grace. May my body reveal fullness through the beauty of holiness and refined expressions of mercy.

I ask for alignment in all these things. May God, Jesus, and the Holy Spirit fill and align me spirit, soul, and body today. May I receive revelation from your Voice and confirmation in your Word. May my mouth always praise You.

Hebrews 12:1-13

So then let's also run the race that is laid out in front of us, since we have such a great cloud of witnesses surrounding us. Let's throw off any extra baggage, get rid of the sin that trips us up, and fix our eyes on Jesus, faith's pioneer and perfecter. He endured the cross, ignoring the shame, for the sake of the joy that was laid out in front of him, and sat down at the right side of God's throne.

Run the race with discipline.

Think about the one who endured such opposition from sinners so that you won't be discouraged and you won't give up. In your struggle against sin, you haven't resisted yet to the point of shedding blood, and you have forgotten the encouragement that addresses you as sons and daughters:

My child, don't make light of the Lord's discipline

or give up when you are corrected by him,

because the Lord disciplines whomever he loves,

and he punishes every son or daughter whom he accepts.

Bear hardship for the sake of discipline. God is treating you like sons and daughters! What child isn't disciplined by his or her father? But if you don't experience discipline, which happens to all children, then you are illegitimate and not real sons and daughters. What's more, we had human parents who disciplined us, and we respected them for it. How much more should we submit to the Father of spirits and live? Our human parents disciplined us for a little while, as it seemed best to them, but God does it for our benefit so that we can share his holiness. No discipline is fun while it lasts, but it seems painful at the time. Later, however, it yields the peaceful fruit of righteousness for those who have been trained by it.

So strengthen your drooping hands and weak knees! Make straight paths for your feet so that if any part is lame, it will be healed rather than injured more seriously.

What is my

why?

Identify your motive.

S a v e d

I call my spirit forward in the name of Jesus, to be blessed and to be honored. The Scriptures say that you are the God who saves with grace, and so I bless myself with vision and purpose.

May my spirit understand the depths of your sight toward me. May my faith rise as I ponder all the ways I am known by your care. May my soul rest in the gentleness of your thoughts about me, and may my mind come into agreement with the way in which you love.

May you give my body the grace to exhibit and express what is known in my heart, that I would reflect in the physical realm what has been made manifest in the spiritual realm. Let me be fulfilled in my salvation, so that I can give from abundance.

I ask for alignment in all these things. May God, Jesus, and the Holy Spirit fill and align me spirit, soul, and body today. May I receive revelation from your Voice and confirmation in your Word. May my mouth always praise You.

Ephesians 2:1-10

It wasn't so long ago that you were mired in that old stagnant life of sin. You let the world, which doesn't know the first thing about living, tell you how to live. You filled your lungs with polluted unbelief, and then exhaled disobedience. We all did it, all of us doing what we felt like doing, when we felt like doing it, all of us in the same boat. It's a wonder God didn't lose his temper and do away with the whole lot of us. Instead, immense in mercy and with an incredible love, he embraced us. He took our sin-dead lives and made us alive in Christ. He did all this on his own, with no help from us! Then he picked us up and set us down in highest heaven in company with Jesus, our Messiah. Now God has us where he wants us, with all the time in this world and the next to shower grace and kindness upon us in Christ Jesus. Saving is all his idea, and all his work. All we do is trust him enough to let him do it. It's God's gift from start to finish!

Worthy

I call my spirit forward in the name of Jesus, to be blessed and to be honored. The Scriptures say that I am my Beloved's and He is mine, and so I bless myself with belonging. This desire for expression is released through creation.

May my spirit be filled with attachment to my Creator. May I rise to meet my Maker with confidence and assurance, that He is for me, with me, and in me. May my soul rest in the presence of love and acceptance. May my mind be still in the oneness of God, gathered and refreshed. May my body move with freedom and mercy as it reflects the wholeness of divine adoration.

I ask for alignment in all these things. May God, Jesus, and the Holy Spirit fill and align me spirit, soul, and body today. May I receive revelation from your Voice and confirmation in your Word. May my mouth always praise You.

Song of Songs 6

[Daughters of Jerusalem]
Which way did your lover go,
you who are the most beautiful of women?
Which way did your lover turn,
that we may look for him along with you?
[Woman]
My lover has gone down to his garden,
to the fragrant plantings,
to graze in the gardens,
to gather the lilies.
I belong to my lover and my lover belongs to me—
the one grazing among the lilies.
An overwhelming sight
[Man]
You are as beautiful, my dearest, as Tirzah,
as lovely as Jerusalem,
formidable as those lofty sights.
Turn your eyes away from me,
for they overwhelm me!
Your hair is like a flock of goats
as they stream down from Gilead.
Your teeth are like a flock of ewes

as they come up from the washing pool—
all of them perfectly matched,
not one of them lacks its twin.
Like a slice of pomegranate is the curve of your face
behind the veil of your hair.
There may be sixty queens
and eighty secondary wives,
young women beyond counting,
but my dove, my perfect one, is one of a kind.
To her mother she's the only one,
radiant to the one who bore her.
Young women see her and declare her fortunate;
queens and secondary wives praise her.
Who is this, gazing down like the morning star,
beautiful as the full moon,
radiant as the sun,
formidable as those lofty sights?
[Man]
To the nut grove I went down
to look upon the fresh growth in the valley,
to see whether the vine was in flower,
whether the pomegranates had bloomed.
I hardly knew myself;
she had set me in an official's chariot!
[Man]
Come back, come back, Shulammite!
Come back, come back, so we may admire you.
How you all admire the Shulammite
as she whirls between two circles of dancers!

Hopeful

I call my spirit forward in the name of Jesus, to be blessed and to be honored. The Scriptures say that you give us a hope and a future, so I bless myself with expectancy. It is in our trust and anticipation of your coming that we develop fulfilled desires like the Tree of Life.

May my spirit be still enough to believe in your hope. May my heart be guided by love as I wait on you and also take steps forward in faith. May my soul be refreshed by the reality of grace in my midst. May my mind be opened to your best plan in my life. May my body be brought into flight as it heals and is refreshed deep down in my bones. May I rest in your plan and in your time.

I ask for alignment in all these things. May God, Jesus, and the Holy Spirit fill and align me spirit, soul, and body today. May I receive revelation from your Voice and confirmation in your Word. May my mouth always praise You.

Psalm 147:11

The Lord delights in those who fear him,
Who put their hope in his unfailing love.

How do I go?

Identify your forms of practical expression.

Courageous

I call my spirit forward in the name of Jesus, to be blessed and to be honored. The Scriptures say to be strong and courageous and not to fear. It is your power and confidence that brings us faith, strength, and victory. You fulfill your promises and your love through trust in your strong hand, and so I bless myself with steadfast faith.

May my spirit be filled with gratitude, bravery, and courage. May I experience your victory and your provision over all my fears. May my mind be consecrated to your promises and your covenant. May my soul be healed from anxiety, unmet needs, and unmerited pain. May I trust in your leadership, in your voice and in your strengthened plan and purpose for my body and health.

I ask for alignment in all these things. May God, Jesus, and the Holy Spirit fill and align me spirit, soul, and body today. May I receive revelation from your Voice and confirmation in your Word. May my mouth always praise You.

Deuteronomy 31:6

Be strong and courageous. Do not fear or be in dread of them, for it is the Lord your God who goes with you. He will not leave you or forsake you."

K i n d

I call my spirit forward in the name of Jesus, to be blessed and to be honored. The Scriptures say that your kindness leads us to repentance. It is your heart and your generosity, even in our sin, that paves a way for our redemption. You fulfill your work in us as you guide us, correct us, and help us turn around, and so I bless myself with kindness.

May my spirit be filled with awareness, honesty, and instruction. May I experience your provision and your understanding in all my circumstances. May my mind be healed of incorrect thinking and hurts. May my soul be made aligned with truth, peace, and strength. May I trust in your heart for me, in your Word and in your joy in my creation.

I ask for alignment in all these things. May God, Jesus, and the Holy Spirit fill and align me spirit, soul, and body today. May I receive revelation from your Voice and confirmation in your Word. May my mouth always praise You.

Romans 2:4

Or do you think lightly of the riches of His kindness and tolerance and patience, not knowing that the kindness of God leads you to repentance?

Grounded

I call my spirit forward in the name of Jesus, to be blessed and to be honored. The Scriptures say we are rooted and grounded in love, and so I bless myself with stillness, balance, and depth.

May my spirit be girded and guarded with faith. May I be blessed with roots that grow as deep into the ground as they go high into the sky. May my soul be magnified by the steadiness of this love. May I be gentle in my manners and sure in my direction. May my body be healed and strengthened by this resolve and this focus.

I ask for alignment in all these things. May God, Jesus, and the Holy Spirit fill and align me spirit, soul, and body today. May I receive revelation from your Voice and confirmation in your Word. May my mouth always praise You.

Ephesians 3:16-20

I pray that out of his glorious riches he may strengthen you with power through his Spirit in your inner being, so that Christ may dwell in your hearts through faith. And I pray that you, being rooted and established in love, may have power, together with all the Lord's holy people, to grasp how wide and long and high and deep is the love of Christ, and to know this love that surpasses knowledge—that you may be filled to the measure of all the fullness of God.

Now to him who is able to do immeasurably more than all we ask or imagine, according to his power that is at work within us, to him be glory in the church and in Christ Jesus throughout all generations, for ever and ever! Amen.

Who is my tribe?

Identify the people you relate to.

H o n e s t

I call my spirit forward in the name of Jesus, to be blessed and to be honored. The Scriptures say to think on whatever is true and noble, and so I bless myself with honesty. It is when we live with integrity that we can understand your heart and your provision over us.

May my spirit be blessed to be humbled, aware, and open to what is true. May I rest in the divinity of that truth while working it out in the humanity of my journey. May I be enlarged with the obedience to be truly me with each step of my walk. May my soul rest in the fact that you are God, and I am not. May my mind be renewed with the joy of your salvation over me. May my body be freed and delivered from the confinement of denial. May it live and move and have joy in imperfect perfection.

I ask for alignment in all these things. May God, Jesus, and the Holy Spirit fill and align me spirit, soul, and body today. May I receive revelation from your Voice and confirmation in your Word. May my mouth always praise You.

Philippians 4:8

Finally, brothers and sisters, whatever is true, whatever is noble, whatever is right, whatever is pure, whatever is lovely, whatever is admirable—if anything is excellent or praiseworthy—think about such things.

Victorious

I call my spirit forward in the name of Jesus, to be blessed and to be honored. The Scriptures say I am more than a conqueror in Christ, and so I bless myself with victory.

May all the weak places within me meet strength. May my heart grow mighty in battle through the power of rest. May I soak deeply in the delight of Presence. May I become the author of my life through the power of my testimony. May my actions be bold and kind, truthful and loving, affectionate and full of grace.

May my mind match with understanding the tenderness of Your heart. May my body move swiftly with steadfastness and poise. May I increase in favor with both God and men.

I ask for alignment in all these things. May God, Jesus, and the Holy Spirit fill and align me spirit, soul, and body today. May I receive revelation from your Voice and confirmation in your Word. May my mouth always praise You.

Romans 8:31-39

So, what do you think? With God on our side like this, how can we lose? If God didn't hesitate to put everything on the line for us, embracing our condition and exposing himself to the worst by sending his own Son, is there anything else he wouldn't gladly and freely do for us? And who would dare tangle with God by messing with one of God's chosen? Who would dare even to point a finger? The One who died for us—who was raised to life for us!—is in the presence of God at this very moment sticking up for us. Do you think anyone is going to be able to drive a wedge between us and Christ's love for us? There is no way! Not trouble, not hard times, not hatred, not hunger, not homelessness, not bullying threats, not backstabbing, not even the worst sins listed in Scripture:

They kill us in cold blood because they hate you.
We're sitting ducks; they pick us off one by one.

None of this fazes us because Jesus loves us. I'm absolutely convinced that nothing—nothing living or dead, angelic or demonic, today or tomorrow, high or low, thinkable or unthinkable— absolutely nothing can get between us and God's love because of the way that Jesus our Master has embraced us.

Strong

I call my spirit forward in the name of Jesus, to be blessed and to be honored. The Scriptures say that you strengthen us with power in our inner beings through your Spirit, so I bless myself with truth. It is in communion with you that we grow, are nourished, are nurtured, and are built into all that we can become.

May my spirit be filled with joy, peace, and unwavering confidence. May I experience your heart and your works in all ways that lead to fruitfulness and abundance. May my mind be girded with truth and passion. May my soul be refreshed by the strength of productivity. May my body flourish as I work and grow in the ways you have set before me.

I ask for alignment in all these things. May God, Jesus, and the Holy Spirit fill and align me spirit, soul, and body today. May I receive revelation from your Voice and confirmation in your Word. May my mouth always praise You.

Ephesians 3:14-21

I pray that out of his glorious riches he may strengthen you with power through his Spirit in your inner being, so that Christ may dwell in your hearts through faith. And I pray that you, being rooted and established in love, may have power, together with all the Lord's holy people, to grasp how wide and long and high and deep is the love of Christ, and to know this love that surpasses knowledge—that you may be filled to the measure of all the fullness of God.

Where can I give?

Identify avenues for charity!

Abundant

I call my spirit forward in the name of Jesus, to be blessed and to be honored. The Scriptures say that you provide immeasurably more than we could ever ask or think, and so I bless myself with abundance. It is your presence that brings us fulfillment, empowerment, and excellence. You fulfill your promises and give us joy greater than we can imagine or do ourselves.

May my spirit be filled with gratitude, faith, and obedience. May I experience your heart for me as I put all my hope in you. May my mind be consecrated to your joy and your faithfulness. May my soul grow in purposeful works, provision of health, and stillness. May I trust in your leadership, in your timing and in your plan as you work all things for my good.

I ask for alignment in all these things. May God, Jesus, and the Holy Spirit fill and align me spirit, soul, and body today. May I receive revelation from your Voice and confirmation in your Word. May my mouth always praise You.

Ephesians 3:20-21

Now to him who is able to do far more abundantly than all that we ask or think, according to the power at work within us, to him be glory in the church and in Christ Jesus throughout all generations, forever and ever. Amen.

Graceful

I call my spirit forward in the name of Jesus, to be blessed and to be honored. The Scriptures say it is by grace we have been saved so that no man can boast, and so I bless myself with humility.

Let everything within me receive and express grace. Let guilt from the past be washed white as snow. May my actions match your deeds as I release my mistakes and advocate for understanding. May your salvation permeate my mind and my thoughts. In this place of surrender, may I gather my healing. May my soul be aligned with truth, for it is finished. May my body resonate with strength because in your death, you gave me wholeness.

I ask for alignment in all these things. May God, Jesus, and the Holy Spirit fill and align me spirit, soul, and body today. May I receive revelation from your Voice and confirmation in your Word. May my mouth always praise You.

Ephesians 2:8-9

Although I am less than the least of all the Lord's people, this grace was given me: to preach to the Gentiles the boundless riches of Christ, and to make plain to everyone the administration of this mystery, which for ages past was kept hidden in God, who created all things.

Surrender

I call my spirit forward in the name of Jesus, to be blessed and to be honored. The Scriptures say that pleasing you requires faith, and so I bless myself with the ability to fall into your grace. It is in our surrender that your perfect peace and power can be made manifest.

May my spirit be blessed with the desire to yield. May my actions and my creativity come from a place of oneness and trust. May my heart be magnified by your filling of me with your divinity.

May my soul work out its salvation with fear and trembling. May I listen to your voice, and may my mind be diligent to align. May my thoughts be those of integrity, wholeheartedness, and sacrifice. May my body be filled with the joy of childlike movement. May my steps be made manifest by your hand.

I ask for alignment in all these things. May God, Jesus, and the Holy Spirit align me spirit, soul, and body today. May I receive revelation from your Voice and confirmation in your Word. May my mouth always praise You.

Hebrews 11:6

And without faith it is impossible to please Him, for he who comes to God must believe that He exists and that He is a rewarder of those who seek Him.

How do I rest?

Identify the best methods for self-care.

S t i l l

I call my spirit forward in the name of Jesus, to be blessed and to be honored. The Scriptures say to be still and know that you are God, so I bless myself with anchored hope. When we are still, we allow you to fight for us, provide for us, and show us your grace.

May my spirit be filled with stillness, quiet love, and unwavering strength. May I experience your heart fill in any weak spots or burdens that I am not intended to carry. May my mind be aligned and refreshed by your work on the cross. May my soul be nourished and rested in your power. May my body flourish as I am healed, restored, and honored.

I ask for alignment in all these things. May God, Jesus, and the Holy Spirit fill and align me spirit, soul, and body today. May I receive revelation from your Voice and confirmation in your Word. May my mouth always praise You.

Psalm 46:10

He says, "Be still, and know that I am God;
I will be exalted among the nations,

I will be exalted in the earth."

Satisfied

I call my spirit forward in the name of Jesus, to be blessed and to be honored. The Scriptures say that your love is better than life, and so I bless myself to be satisfied in you. It is your presence that brings us hope, joy, and peace. You fulfill your promises and your love through ache and also through contentment.

May my spirit be filled with gratitude, awareness, and sight. May I experience your intent and your provision for all my needs. May my mind be consecrated to your goodness and your faithfulness. May my soul be healed from disappointment, unmet longing, and unmerited suffering. May I trust in your leadership, in your timing and in your perfect outcome for my life and body.

I ask for alignment in all these things. May God, Jesus, and the Holy Spirit fill and align me spirit, soul, and body today. May I receive revelation from your Voice and confirmation in your Word. May my mouth always praise You.

Psalm 63:1-5

A psalm of David. When he was in the Desert of Judah.

You, God, are my God,
earnestly I seek you;
I thirst for you,
my whole being longs for you,
in a dry and parched land
where there is no water.

I have seen you in the sanctuary

and beheld your power and your glory.

Because your love is better than life,

my lips will glorify you.

I will praise you as long as I live,

and in your name I will lift up my hands.

I will be fully satisfied as with the richest of foods;

with singing lips my mouth will praise you.

Fearless

I call my spirit forward in the name of Jesus, to be blessed and to be honored. The Scriptures say that perfect love casts out fear, and so I bless myself with faith.

May my spirit come into full rest because your hand is peace. May I delight in knowing that when I am still, I invite you to be God in my life. May my soul give itself the space to accept this type of courage. May my heart be guided by gentleness and truth. May my body be released of its worries and tension. May it heal inside-out by this gift that is grace.

I ask for alignment in all these things. May God, Jesus, and the Holy Spirit fill and align me spirit, soul, and body today. May I receive revelation from your Voice and confirmation in your Word. May my mouth always praise You.

1 John 4:18

Such love has no fear, because perfect love expels all fear. If we are afraid, it is for fear of punishment, and this shows that we have not fully experienced his perfect love.

How do I move?

Identify your most refreshing forms of exercise.

Becoming

I call my spirit forward in the name of Jesus, to be blessed and to be honored. The Scriptures say that the old passes away and the new has come, and so I bless myself in becoming. It's in the transformation from what was to what will be that we find ourselves in you.

May my spirit be blessed to pursue your will. May my initiation into creativity and inspiration be birthed in your time and presence. May I rest into your care as you make the miraculous come alive in me.

May my soul breathe in new desires as it aligns to your power and righteousness. May my thoughts line up with the joy of your heart, and may my actions give way to the purity in arriving. May my body come forth to be alive and well and release its motion as it blooms.

I ask for alignment in all these things. May God, Jesus, and the Holy Spirit align me spirit, soul, and body today. May I receive revelation from your Voice and confirmation in your Word. May my mouth always praise You.

Romans 12:2

And do not be conformed to this world, but be transformed by the renewing of your mind, so that you may prove what the will of God is, that which is good and acceptable and perfect.

A l i v e

I call my spirit forward in the name of Jesus, to be blessed and to be honored. The Scriptures say to live is Christ, to die is gain. And so I bless myself with resurrection life.

May my spirit drink of the fullness of the Trinity. With ease and with grace, may I be nurtured and nourished. Dry bones come back to life in Christ; so may the weakened parts of my mind be brought into alignment and Christlikeness. May my body rejoice in movement, and may my physicality be cleared, healed, and infused with the blood of Jesus.

I ask for alignment in all these things. May God, Jesus, and the Holy Spirit fill and align me spirit, soul, and body today. May I receive revelation from your Voice and confirmation in your Word. May my mouth always praise You.

Philippians 1:12-27

Brothers and sisters, I want you to know that the things that have happened to me have actually advanced the gospel. The whole Praetorian Guard and everyone else knows that I'm in prison for Christ. Most of the brothers and sisters have had more confidence through the Lord to speak the word boldly and bravely because of my jail time. Some certainly preach Christ with jealous and competitive motives, but others preach with good motives. They are motivated by love, because they know that I'm put here to give a defense of the gospel; the others preach Christ because of their selfish ambition. They are insincere, hoping to cause me more pain while I'm in prison.

What do I think about this? Just this: since Christ is proclaimed in every possible way, whether from dishonest or true motives, I'm glad and I'll continue to be glad. I'm glad because I know that this will result in my release through your prayers and the help of the Spirit of Jesus Christ. It is my expectation and hope that I won't be put to shame in anything. Rather, I hope with daring courage that Christ's greatness will be seen in my body, now as always, whether I live or die. Because for me, living serves Christ and dying is even better. If I continue to live in this world, I get results from my work. But I don't know what I prefer. I'm torn between the two because I want to leave this life and be with Christ, which is far better. However, it's more important for me to stay in this world for your sake. I'm sure of this: I will stay alive and remain with all of you to help your progress and the joy of your faith, and to increase your pride in Christ Jesus through my presence when I visit you again.

Most important, live together in a manner worthy of Christ's gospel.

Sanctified

I call my spirit forward in the name of Jesus, to be blessed and to be honored. The Scriptures say that we are sanctified by the offering of your body for us, and so I bless myself with the joy of being set apart. When we are chosen, we surrender our lives in all ways, shapes, and forms.

May my spirit be filled with stillness, holiness, and unwavering faith. May I experience your love to carry the fulfillment of the calling you've given me. May my mind be preserved and inspired by your work on the cross. May my soul be rested and and motivated by your heart. May my body flourish as I dedicate it fully to your care.

I ask for alignment in all these things. May God, Jesus, and the Holy Spirit fill and align me spirit, soul, and body today. May I receive revelation from your Voice and confirmation in your Word. May my mouth always praise You.

Hebrews 10:10

And by that will we have been sanctified through the offering of the body of Jesus Christ once for all.

How do I pray

and persevere?

Identify your best strategy for alignment to God.

Prayerful

I call my spirit forward in the name of Jesus, to be blessed and to be honored. The Scriptures say to rejoice always, to pray without ceasing, and to give thanks in all circumstances. And so I bless myself with the grace and power of intercession.

May my spirit rise above all circumstances, and may it always live to give you praise. May I believe in your goodness toward me and for me, and may I always be alive to your Spirit living in me. May my soul release the words and groans of prayer, even when I feel empty or without a voice. May my mind come into form as it agrees with you in intercession. May my body heal and release healing as fulfillment is made between Heaven and Earth, my future and my past. May my Present reflect your Presence.

I ask for alignment in all these things. May God, Jesus, and the Holy Spirit fill and align me spirit, soul, and body today. May I receive revelation from your Voice and confirmation in your Word. May my mouth always praise You.

1 Thessalonians 5:12-24

We ask you, Christian brothers, to respect those who work among you. The Lord has placed them over you and they are your teachers. You must think much of them and love them because of their work. Live in peace with each other.

We ask you, Christian brothers, speak to those who do not want to work. Comfort those who feel they cannot keep going on. Help the weak. Understand and be willing to wait for all men. Do not let anyone pay back for the bad he received. But look for ways to do good to each other and to all people.

Be full of joy all the time. Never stop praying. In everything give thanks. This is what God wants you to do because of Christ Jesus. Do not try to stop the work of the Holy Spirit. Do not laugh at those who speak for God. Test everything and do not let good things get away from you. Keep away from everything that even looks like sin.

May the God of peace set you apart for Himself. May every part of you be set apart for God. May your spirit and your soul and your body be kept complete. May you be without blame when our Lord Jesus Christ comes again. The One Who called you is faithful and will do what He promised.

Intimate

I call my spirit forward in the name of Jesus, to be blessed and to be honored. The Scriptures say you share great and hidden things when we call to you, so I bless myself with desire.

May my spirit be guided by your righteous love for me, and may I long for the security of intimacy and legitimacy. May I endure the stillness that brings peace and lasting joy. May my soul be quiet in vulnerability and be awakened to the deeper places of love. May my mind receive the freedom that comes with true life. May my body rejoice in the healing and fulfillment that intimacy offers.

I ask for alignment in all these things. May God, Jesus, and the Holy Spirit fill and align me spirit, soul, and body today. May I receive revelation from your Voice and confirmation in your Word. May my mouth always praise You.

Jeremiah 33:3

Call to me and I will answer you, and will tell you great and hidden things that you have not known.

Gratitude

I call my spirit forward in the name of Jesus, to be blessed and to be honored. The Scriptures say that a thankful heart is a happy heart, and so I bless myself with gratitude.

Let everything within me sing with thanks. Let old thoughts turn into new perspectives. May suffering result in the deepest joy. May my needs be met with the simplest of touch. In this place of praise, may my heart understand your sacrifice. May my soul understand your peace. May my body resonate with gratitude because you paid to give me both--humility and fulfillment.

I ask for alignment in all these things. May God, Jesus, and the Holy Spirit fill and align me spirit, soul, and body today. May I receive revelation from your Voice and confirmation in your Word. May my mouth always praise You.

Psalm 138

I give thanks to you with all my heart, Lord.
I sing your praise before all other gods.
I bow toward your holy temple
and thank your name
for your loyal love and faithfulness
because you have made your name and word
greater than everything else.
On the day I cried out, you answered me.
You encouraged me with inner strength.
Let all the earth's rulers give thanks to you, Lord,
when they hear what you say.
Let them sing about the Lord's ways
because the Lord's glory is so great!
Even though the Lord is high,
he can still see the lowly,
but God keeps his distance from the arrogant.
Whenever I am in deep trouble,
you make me live again;
you send your power against my enemies' wrath;
you save me with your strong hand.
The Lord will do all this for my sake.
Your faithful love lasts forever, Lord!
Don't let go of what your hands
have made.

"Father, Son, and Holy Spirit-- align me spirit, soul, and body today. Fill me afresh with revelation from Your heart and confirmation in your Word."

Made in the USA
Columbia, SC
28 September 2018